A BOX OF PANDORAS

By Steve Brewer

Chapter 1

When I first heard that my film idol was coming to New Mexico, you could've knocked me over with a feather boa.

Funny that it was Inez Hidalgo who gave me the news. Inez could not possibly care less about celebrities. She runs the Bluebird Motor Inn here in Pandora, and she's a very practical person. We've been friends since grade school and I love her to death, but she's always treated my devotion to the International Michael Girard Fan Club as a sort of *affliction* that prevents me from enjoying everyday life to its fullest.

That is complete horse manure, as I enjoy life as much as anyone I know. I have a natural exuberance that I consider one of my best qualities, right up there with my still-shapely legs and my naturally curly auburn hair. My husband, Harley, is correct when he calls me a "force of nature," even if he doesn't always mean it in a kind way.

When Inez called, I was busy affixing address labels to fan club newsletters. My fingers were sticky, so I used a ballpoint pen to answer the ring-tone (a jazzy trumpet version of "Happy Days Are Here Again") and put her on the speaker.

"Loretta! Turn on your TV!"

"What?"

"Turn on the noon news! Channel Seven!"

I knew it must be something big. Inez is not the excitable type.

"Aww," she said. "Too late. They're going to the next story."

"What happened?"

"Nothing."

"Have you lost your ever-loving--"

"But something's *gonna* happen. Your boyfriend's coming to Santa Fe."

She was trying to tweak me, as I most certainly do not have a "boyfriend," but I instantly knew she meant Michael Girard. My breath caught in my throat.

"They're starting a new film festival next month," she said. "He's the guest of honor."

I was so glad Inez couldn't see me, a full-grown woman nearly fifty years old, gasping and gulping like a goldfish. I finally managed to sputter: "I need to call Harley."

"Of course you do. He'll *love* to hear this."

"Thanks, Inez. Talk soon."

I turned off the phone with my elbow, then went to the kitchen to wash the goo off my trembling hands. I stood at the sink a long time, getting my breathing under control.

The front of our house overlooks Red Mesa and the twinkling bowl of lights that is our hometown, but from the kitchen window all you see is dry prairie studded with cactus, fence posts and the occasional black cow. A daily reminder of why I'd spent my youth fantasizing about escape.

Popcorn matinees at Pandora's lone cinema, the Bijou, had shown me there could be more to life than small towns and cows and worrying about rain. Life could be lived with sophistication and style. That's why I fixated on Michael Girard when I was a teen. He seemed so cosmopolitan compared to the cowpokes and country boys who populated Pandora. He embodied a glamorous, faraway world.

Now he was coming to my world. Santa Fe is only a three-hour drive from Pandora. (In New Mexico, *everywhere* is a three-hour drive. You get used to it.) And while Santa Fe, with its celebrities and artistes, seems a different planet from the one I inhabit, it is in fact part of the *same state*, and Mr. Girard would be here soon. Arrangements must be made.

I try not to call my husband at work. He's a busy man, running the feed-and-hardware store that's been in his family for three generations. It's a complicated business with lots of paperwork, so Harley's brain is usually occupied with inventory and special orders and which taciturn rancher needs a new windmill vane. A call from me can derail his train of thought and that is not, as he frequently explains, good for business.

But this was big news. The biggest. Michael Girard was coming to Santa Fe, and I would be there to see him, come hell or high water.

I talk fast when I'm excited, and apparently I was babbling because Harley kept instructing me to "settle down," which didn't help. He finally absorbed what I was trying to tell him, and said of course I could attend this film festival he'd never heard of five minutes ago. Isn't he great?

To get me off the phone, Harley urged me to get details about the festival and give him a full report at dinner. I hung up, letting him get back to his wingnuts and whatnot, and hurried to my computer.

You might not think of rural New Mexico as an Internet-savvy place, but that would show how little you know. We've got Wi-Fi here in Pandora, and most homes have at least one computer. I manage the International Michael Girard Fan Club website from my laptop, and it looks as slick and up-to-date as websites designed by professionals, if I do say so myself.

(I learned computer skills at Staked Plains Community College. I take lots of classes there, mostly in the Arts and Humanities. Always trying to improve my mind.)

My laptop usually lives on a desk in my "office," a spare bedroom that's home to the Official International Michael Girard Archives: Fourteen file cabinets full of posters, newspaper clippings and memorabilia, plus videos of all forty-three of Mr. Girard's theatrical releases, including such (deservedly) hard-to-find rarities as "Hammerhead!" and "Travels with Pooky," and the complete first two seasons of the prime-time drama "Empire" before Mr. Girard was replaced in the lead role by Roger Sherwood (that rat).

A quick Google search revealed that the new film festival would be based at the Zia Theater, a 1930s movie palace recently renovated by the state tourism department. A group called the Santa Fe Silver Screen Society (SFSSS) had rented the Zia for the event, and named as director a local theatrical type named Andre de Carlo. I had to read that guy's name about ten times (the festival was his "brainchild," blah, blah) before I got down to the real news: Michael Girard had indeed agreed to attend and accept accolades. Sweet Jesus, I nearly swooned when I saw his name there in black-and-white.

Mr. Girard wasn't the only big-name celebrity, either. Ava Andrews, his co-star on "Empire," would attend the festival, and there were rumors of a cameo appearance by Roger Sherwood (that rat). Lots of stars have vacation homes around Santa Fe, so no telling who else might show up.

I was so excited, it was all I could do not to call Harley again. Instead, I called Inez and squealed at her for five minutes, while she pretended to care. When she finally got a word in edgewise, she said, "So, you're going, right?"

"Oh, absolutely. This is an opportunity that cannot be missed, no matter the cost."

"You sound like you're rehearsing for Harley."

"Not at all," I said. "You know how understanding he's always been about my devotion to Mr. Girard."

"More than I ever would've been, if I were in his shoes."

"So you've said. But Harley is not the problem here. It's you."

"Me? How am I the problem? You wouldn't even know about this film festival if I hadn't called."

"I want you to go with me."

Long pause.

"You're kidding, right?"

"Come on, Inez. It'll be fun. And you deserve a vacation."

"There is no way in hell I could get away from the motel for -- how long is it?"

"We'd have to come back on a Sunday. So, four days altogether."

"Four days. I can barely go four *hours* without something going wrong around here."

"But I don't want to go by myself," I whined. "I won't know anybody there."

"Take Harley."

"He won't go. He hates this kind of thing."

"How do you know? It's not like this has ever come up before. Why don't you ask him?"

"He'd have to dress up. Maybe even wear a tuxedo. He'd never go for that."

"Girl, that man will do anything you ask. Always been that way, and it always will be so."

"That makes me a lucky woman."

"Makes you spoiled, though."

That stung. Inez and her plain-spoken ways. Why is your best friend always your harshest critic?

"Make Harley his favorite dinner," she said. "Sweet-talk him. A little kissy-face. You'll get what you want."

"Come on, Inez."

She laughed. "I think Harley will look good in a tux."

Chapter 2

Harley *did* look good in a tux. Who knew? He'd never worn one before. Of course, a man has to be built like an absolute tree stump to look bad in a tuxedo. Harley is a little on the plump side, but the tux fit great.

He surprised me by buying it from eBay. I mean, the eBay part didn't surprise me. Harley *loves* to buy and sell items online. Such horse-trading appeals to his mercantile nature. But I'd assumed he'd *rent* a tux. Once he came around to the idea of accompanying me to the film festival (which took only two weeks of cuddly persuasion), he decided to buy a tux for the opening night gala. He'd likely need a tux anyway, he said, for our children's weddings. Ben and Jessica are studying at the University of New Mexico, and neither currently seems inclined toward matrimony, but Harley likes to plan ahead.

The day the tux arrived via UPS, he tried it on as soon as he got home from work. I think the seller must've worn it only once for a wedding or a funeral or something because it was like brand-new.

While Harley has been known to wear a full suit-and-tie on special occasions, his weekday attire consists of short-sleeve gray coveralls, which don't show dirt and which he prefers over jeans because he does a lot of bending over at work and he's very conscious of the plumber's cleavage issue at KIMBALLS.

(I always think of the store in all-caps because of the apostrophe-free KIMBALLS sign that Harley's dad paid ten thousand dollars to have erected over the store thirty years ago. You can see that glowing orange sign from all over town. Harley keeps threatening to replace it, especially around Halloween, when vandals annually damage the sign so it reads BALLS, but he always has it repaired instead. In memory of his dad, I guess.)

I followed Harley into the bedroom and fussed over him while he put on the tuxedo and figured out the studs and cufflinks and cummerbund. This took longer than you might think, considering that we are both reasonably intelligent adults with better-than-average motor skills. But the garment did not come with instructions.

Once he was all put together, Harley stood before the full-length mirror, flushing and pushing up his gold-rimmed glasses.

"It'll look better when I have shoes on," he said.

"You look great, sweetie. Taller, somehow, and really trim. There's a reason men stick with traditional formalwear. Black is very slimming."

"Probably fit better if I'd drop a few pounds."

"It fits fine. You look very classy. People will think I showed up on the arm of a celebrity."

He straightened his tie. "I feel like Count Chocula."

"Hush, before I pour milk on you."

We managed a hug and a kiss without creasing his new clothes. Wifely approval given, I started to pull away, but Harley held onto my shoulders.

"Hate to tell you this, hon," he said. "But I've got bad news."

"Who died? Was it Ruth Bradshaw? I knew she was hanging by a thread, but LouAnn tried to tell me that she--"

"No, no, nothing like that. Old Lady Bradshaw is still kicking, as far as I know."

"Not for long, the way I hear it. Morton Greems over at the mortuary already special-ordered her casket. Pink satin interior. Hot pink! Who ever heard of such a thing?"

"Loretta!"

"What?"

"I'm not talking about that."

"Well, there's no need to yell."

He sighed. "It's Mitzi Tyner. She came in the store today."

No wonder Harley was so hesitant to speak. He knew the mere mention of Mitzi's name made me want to spit.

My entire life, Mitzi Tyner has stood in my way. We were in the same grade all through school (though she is older and already *had* her fiftieth birthday, while mine's still months away), and Mitzi was Miss Everything-All-the-Time. Beauty queen. Homecoming queen. Rodeo queen. Class president. Head cheerleader for the Pandora High School Boxers (dogs, not underwear). Editor of the school newspaper, The Boxer Bulletin, when she can barely write her own name.

I never got to be any of those things. No, my ambitions always were thwarted by the raven hair, bouncing bosom and blinding smile of Mitzi Tyner. Every boy in school would vote for her for *anything*, as long as she showed up every day in her tight sweaters and snug skirts. Feeding their adolescent fantasies. Happily supplying the entire town with wet dreams.

I thought it would end after school, but Mitzi continues to follow me around town, thwarting me. If I join a civic organization such as the Save Route 66 Committee or the Association to Beautify Pandora Creek, Mitzi immediately joins, too, and is inevitably elected president within weeks. She's president of everything in town. Not that she ever does any *work*, mind you. That's left to volunteers like me. Mitzi apparently believes her role as a community leader is to stand around and be admired, and the townspeople of Pandora just lap that up with a spoon. I swear, sometimes I think the only reason Mitzi joined the Presbyterian Church was so she could head up the Ladies Auxiliary and boss me around.

"What did Mitzi want?"

"We got to talking," he said. "You know how she is. And she told me she'd heard about the film festival."

"Oh, no."

"I'm sorry, hon. But she's signed up to attend."

"No! She'll *ruin* it!"

"Now, come on, Loretta, there's no way--"

"She ruins *everything*. She knows how much Mr. Girard means to me. That's why she's sticking her big nose into--"

"She acted like she didn't even know we were going," Harley said. "Like she was telling me to make sure you'd heard about it."

"Such a liar! She knows we're going. That's the only reason she wants to be there. She doesn't care anything about film or Mr. Girard. She's hoping for the chance to embarrass me somehow, to steal my thunder. I can't believe she would try to horn in--"

"She can't ruin it for you unless you let her," Harley said.

"Oh, that's what you always say! Next thing you know, she's the president of the Pandora Garden Society and I'm the one shoveling manure."

"No manure at a film festival," he said. "Not the kind you shovel, anyway."

"Don't try to distract me with your boundless wit, Harley. Every time the spotlight falls on me, Mitzi Tyner pushes me out of the way. Remember the talent show in high school?"

"Good Lord, don't start on that, Loretta. That was thirty years ago!"

"Thirty-two. But that's not the point. Mitzi will find a way to make this festival all about her. Everything is about her, all the time. I can't stand it."

My vision blurred. Harley hates when I cry, and he tried to hug me up, but I kept him at arms-length. I didn't want to soil his tuxedo.

"It's good that you told me," I sniffled. "It's good that I know. I can make a plan."

"There you go."

"Lots of time between now and the film festival for her to have an 'accident.'"

"Not funny, Loretta."

"At least I'll have you along to watch my back. Mitzi will be all alone. It's not like Long John would go to Santa Fe with her."

Mitzi's husband, Long John Tyner, owns the Chevrolet dealership overlooking Pandora's main freeway exit. He's a tall, dour man who does nothing but work, but he had what Mitzi needed in a husband -- he was loaded.

Harley winced. "Yeah, that's the other bad news. I was getting to that."

"There's more?"

"Mitzi wanted a roommate, so she's paying Nannette's way."

"No, no! Not Nannette!"

Inviting Nannette Hoch to a film festival was like inviting the Grim Reaper to a birthday party. No one in the whole world is more determined to be unhappy than Nannette

Hoch, and she's made it her mission to take the rest of us down with her.

Granted, she's had a hard life. Nannette was widowed before she was thirty, and some women don't bounce back from a tragedy like that. It didn't help that her husband died under mysterious circumstances. Some believed Augie Hoch drove his John Deere tractor into that stock pond on purpose rather than spend another day with Nannette. I prefer to take the charitable view, and consider it a tragic accident.

However it happened, Augie's death sank Nannette like a paper boat. She'd always been a sour person, frowning at the world, and she wrapped herself in church work and drab clothes and pessimism. She was a bitter eighty-year-old widow living in the body of a mousy fifty-year-old.

She was, however, the perfect companion for Mitzi Tyner. Mitzi didn't want a *friend.* She wants an audience. Mitzi and Nannette. Sounds like a couple of French poodles, doesn't it? That's how they act, too. Two snobs mincing about, yipping and yapping and--

"Loretta? Are you all right, hon?"

I snapped back to my own bedroom. The familiar comforter, quilted of my favorite colors -- red and purple and sunny yellow. My vanity table, covered in makeup and hairbrushes and lipstick samples. My loving husband, standing next to our marital bed, wringing his hands.

"You poor, sweet man. Bringing me the bad news rather than letting me hear it on my own."

"Takes courage."

"I know, Harley. You've got plenty of that."

He grinned.

"Now shake off this whole thing with Mitzi," he said. "It doesn't matter. You're going to be the belle of the ball, and you're gonna have *this*--" He ran his hands up and down his tuxedoed torso. "--for your escort. No way Mitzi can top that."

I swallowed my objections and worked up a smile. The man had bought a used tuxedo over eBay just to make me happy. Least I could do was try to make him happy back.

"We'll look great," I said. "And we'll hang out with the VIPs, while Mitzi and Nannette stand in line with the hoi polloi."

"Mitzi will be green with envy."

"Oh, Harley. You always know how to say just the right thing."

Chapter 3

In the days leading up to the film festival, I mostly stayed home. I didn't want to run into Mitzi somewhere and end up making headlines in the weekly Llano County *Headlight*. Half the people in Pandora already think I'm some kind of crackpot for devoting so much uncompensated time and effort to the International Michael Girard Fan Club. I don't need to convince the other half.

Avoiding Mitzi meant that I missed the monthly Garden Society meeting, but, what the hell, it was March, and the only thing growing this time of year was frost.

People have lots of romantic notions about New Mexico, but they're usually not thinking about our part of the state. The high desert between Albuquerque and Amarillo is essentially vacant, except for a few burgs like Pandora strung along Interstate 40. Lots of acreage, lots of sky, lots of cows. Not many people.

The settlers who did homestead out here were always on the lookout for anything to break the relentless wind that goes sweeping 'cross the plain every damn day of the year. That's why Pandora grew around the eroded base of Red Mesa. To travelers on old Route 66, the motor courts and diners tucked beneath that sandstone outcrop must've seemed an oasis.

(That's how my parents met. My mother's family was from Alabama, and they packed into a Studebaker for a driving vacation to the Grand Canyon. Car trouble resulted in a two-night stay in Pandora, where my mother fell for the handsome young mechanic. I've still got a slew of relatives in Alabama. We keep in touch via Facebook.)

I am, of course, too young to remember the days before the interstate highway replaced Route 66. Even when I was a child, neon-lit businesses like the Bijou, Arrowhead Mercantile and the Roadrunner Drive-In already seemed retro, kind of kitschy, though people weren't done using them yet. I can only imagine how it must feel to today's kids. No wonder so many of them go off to college and never return.

We had one shot of fame here in Pandora. Years ago, New Mexico's governor, Bruce King, beloved for his cowboy malapropisms, spouted that a legislative proposal would "open a whole box of Pandoras." Reporters seized on the governor's goof and the story went nationwide. Next thing we knew, network news crews roamed the gusty streets of Pandora, winkingly asking residents what they thought of the ills of the world.

(Some people around here still haven't forgiven old Claude Winesap for appearing on TV with a jawful of chewing tobacco, making us all look like a bunch of hicks.)

Anyhow, out here on the high plains, blustery March is a good month to stay hunkered indoors. I spent a ridiculous amount of time during those weeks in front of the full-length mirror in our bedroom, turning this way and that, studying which of my clothes would do the best job of hiding the twenty pounds of motherhood that still clung to my hips.

Don't know why I even bothered. Whatever I came up with, however elegant I might look, I would be outdone by Mitzi Tyner and her uncanny sense for one-upmanship. Mitzi already owned a grand wardrobe, she had unlimited funds and she had a fearless sense of style. How was I to compete? It was discouraging.

Harley makes a decent living at KIMBALLS, one that has allowed me to pour all my energies into volunteer work and raising our kids, but we're not rolling in dough like Long John Tyner. Four days in Santa Fe would cost a fortune (the hotel alone was three hundred dollars a night!), and I didn't need to make things worse by bloating the credit cards with new clothes.

One exception: I did find a lovely dress to wear to the opening night gala. Inez and I drove to Albuquerque one day for shopping. She hit Costco for cleaning supplies and toilet paper for the motel. I hit the mall to try on gowns. We don't need to go into how long it took. Let's just say that by the end of the day, my arms were chafed from pulling dresses over my head.

Inez was very patient with me, though she didn't shilly-shally about her opinions. Some samples:

"That's not your color. I don't know whose color that is."

"Too much cleavage."

"Too much leg."

"Now you look like a nun."

"You look like you're wearing bedroom drapes."

"Now you look like you're wearing the bed."

"Take it off, quickly. My eyes, my eyes!"

Very helpful. Not.

I finally settled on a gown that I found in a cute little shop called Promenade. Floor-length, emerald-green brocade, snug around the bodice, but drapey around the hips. Narrow straps that mostly left my shoulders bare, but it came with a matching wrap to stay warm.

As I admired the dress in a mirror, I said, "The color sets off my green eyes."

Inez said, "You look like you're going to the prom."

"I *feel* like I'm going to the prom."

I turned sideways, checking for tummy bulge. "You think it's too much?"

"It'll do," Inez said, looking at her watch. "Better than those bridesmaid dresses you were trying on earlier. Buy it. We've got a three-hour drive home."

Later, I told Harley that Inez was rushing me and that's why I spent so much on that dress, but he didn't seem to care. I modeled the gown for him there at home, and he got all pop-eyed and sweaty. Just the effect I was going for.

I may be a little heavier these days, but I'm still five-foot-eight, tall enough that, when I was in my teens, folks were always urging me to become a model. Flattering, but then I met some real models, and they all seemed to be space aliens from the Starvation Galaxy, and I knew that wasn't for me. But height does have its advantages. I put on heels and the right dress, and I stop looking like a soccer mom and look, dare I say it, a little glamorous.

Other than the gown, I kept it casual, using clothes I already owned. This was Santa Fe, after all, not the Academy Awards. And at a film festival, you spend much of the time sitting in the dark. I packed jeans and turtlenecks and blazers. A couple of scarves for windy days. Comfortable walking shoes, as well as the three-inch heels that went with the emerald gown. I'd look my best on opening night, but the rest of the time I'd look like myself.

I packed Harley's suitcase, too. (I consider it a mark of a successful marriage that he would allow me to pick his clothes for such a special trip. Also, if I left it up to him, he'd wear his gray coveralls. People would mistake him for the janitor.) For him: jeans and warm shirts and a black wool coat I bought him two Christmases ago, but which he never wears because he's afraid he'll get something on it. Cowboy boots, of course. That's all Harley ever wears. The shiny loafers that came with the tux made him cringe, but he never said a word against them.

I packed and repacked, always with an eye toward fitting in with the film festival crowd. The thing I feared most was that we'd say or do something to make us seem like small-town goobers. Better to pack light and dress quietly. Park our muddy Suburban out of sight of the swanky hotel. Act like we belonged.

Mitzi Tyner could use a lesson in such social camouflage. With her teased hair and gaudy jewelry, she always displays the fashion sense of a once-and-future rodeo queen.

I heard rumblings, of course. Mitzi blabbed about her shopping sprees so much that most women in Pandora could describe exactly what she planned to wear. They burned up the phone lines, reporting in to me, but I acted like I didn't care in the least. I can take the high road.

What I knew from the gossip was that Mitzi had done her shopping in Santa Fe, not Albuquerque, and had gone completely over the top: Broomstick skirts and embroidered shirts and bolero jackets. Even -- get this -- a flat-brimmed gaucho hat.

I could hardly wait.

FAN FAIR: THE OFFICIAL WEBSITE OF THE
INTERNATIONAL MICHAEL GIRARD FAN CLUB

3:30 p.m. March 20

From the President:

Great news! I just got off the phone with Mr. Girard's personal assistant, Hilda Schmidt, and she has arranged for a face-to-face interview with our favorite actor!

As reported here earlier, Mr. Girard is guest of honor next weekend at the Santa Fe Silver Screen Society Film Festival, and we fans are delighted that he's finally getting the recognition he deserves.

Throughout his forty-year career, Mr. Girard repeatedly has been passed over for such honors as the Oscars and the Emmys, despite doing stellar work in film and on TV. The organizers of this new film festival clearly saw past all the Hollywood politics, and recognize that he'd be a huge draw.

I've met our idol twice before, each time coming away with fond memories and autographed photos (he has lovely penmanship), but we never got a chance to really *talk*. That will change next weekend. As guest of honor, Mr. Girard will be incredibly busy, but dear, sweet Hilda has arranged for an *hour*-long interview about his life, career and plans for the future. I'll tape the interview, so I can present a full transcript here on the website.

Updates and photos to come!

Sincerely,

Loretta Kimball, president, IMGFC

Chapter 4

Santa Fe has grown by leaps and bounds since it was "discovered" thirty years ago by Hollywood moguls and New York *fashionistas*. Now, you start seeing suburbs when you're still ten miles from the historic downtown.

Houses and other buildings in Santa Fe are required by law to look as if they're made of mud. A city of seventy thousand people, the state *capital*, but it resembles a vast indigenous village, sprouted up from the dirt. That adobe fantasy is what tourists pay to see, and "The City Different" gives it to them in spades. A downtown shop can sell the same overpriced junk you'd find in any tourist trap, but if the storefront is covered by a layer of tan stucco, that makes it *exotic*. Go figure.

The historic district does have its charms, even in March when the trees are naked and a brisk wind whips along the streets. The Palace of the Governors, with its long *portal*, where Native American vendors huddle in blankets, offering silver jewelry to throngs of shoppers. St. Francis Cathedral, with its twin stone towers and European design, still looking oddly out of place after more than a century in the same spot. The grand old hotel, La Fonda, and the Inn at Loretto, both stacked like ancient pueblos. The sleek Georgia O'Keeffe Museum. All within a block or two of the central plaza with its obelisk and its gazebo and its brightly plumaged tourists.

Harley poked along in traffic, making the circuit around the plaza so I could sightsee from the warmth of our Chevy Suburban. I bounced in the passenger seat like a child, yapping and pointing out buildings we've seen plenty of times before. Of special interest was the Zia Theater, where the film festival would take place.

"Slow down, Harley!" I shouted as we neared the theater.

"If I go any slower, I'll be going backward."

As if to prove him right, a car behind us honked. Harley ignored the noise, creeping along at the same pace.

The Zia's outer architecture is Southwestern, of course, and does appear to be made of mud, but closer inspection shows artistic touches in colored terra cotta -- sculpted cow skulls, arrowheads, *kachina* dancers and, of course, *zias*, which are simple sun shapes like the red one that graces our yellow state flag. All the decorations were lovingly preserved during the recent renovation. I could hardly wait to see the interior.

After some more honking, Harley turned onto a side street and we found the Hotel Kokopelli two blocks away. Hardly any room in front for unloading, but Harley wedged our Suburban into the narrow driveway that looped past the entry, and got out to speak with a valet.

Kokopelli is another emblem you see all over New Mexico, a Native American fertility symbol, usually depicted as

27

a hunchbacked flute player. A ten-foot-tall metal depiction of Kokopelli was set into the wall above the hotel's entry courtyard. The iron had rusted and streaked the stucco below. The streaks made it look as if the flute player was blasting off into space.

The hotel was done in what's known as Pueblo Revival style, which means its stucco resembles *melting* mud. The hotel was fairly new, but had been built to look extra melty. Made me think of a sand castle, and not in a good way.

Harley popped open my door and said, "Go ahead and get out. I'll get the bags."

"But we're blocking the whole entrance, Harley."

"That's why we should hurry."

"Oh. Okay."

I gathered up my purse and my scarf and checked my lipstick in the sun-visor mirror. By the time I was ready to descend from the passenger seat, Harley had all four of our soft-sided suitcases lined up on the sidewalk like big black prunes. He gave his keys to a valet who looked twelve years old, and the kid climbed into the driver's seat and backed right out into traffic (I closed my eyes) and screeched away.

"Think we'll ever see our Suburban again?"

"Who knows?" Harley said as he gathered up our prunes. "Long as I don't have to find a place to park it."

"Did that kid even work for the hotel? Maybe he's a car thief."

"If he wants our muddy old Suburban, he's welcome to it."

"Well, I don't know about that. We'll want to go home eventually."

Harley had a bag squished under either arm and another dangling from his left hand. He struggled to bend down far enough to pick up the fourth bag. The tail of his plaid shirt was hanging out in the back.

"Want some help carrying those?"

"I got 'em. Just hold the door open."

The cool breeze sent my scarf fluttering over my face, but I emerged unscathed and tugged open the lobby door so Harley could sidle through with our luggage.

Punched-tin chandeliers dangled from the lobby's high ceiling, and the carved front desk looked as if it belonged on the altar of a Spanish church. R.C. Gorman paintings of fat pueblo women adorned the walls, and a bronze Kokopelli danced in the center of a decorative fountain, water spouting from his flute.

The lobby's tile floors and whitewashed walls echoed with the hubbub and hobnob of perhaps forty people. Not in line for the front desk or anything. Just milling around. They were an odd-looking bunch, with lots of tattoos and goatees and fishnet hose and battered cowboy boots. I assumed they were all connected in some way to the film festival.

A wispy bellhop in a black vest sprang out of the crowd.

"Welcome to the Hotel Kokopelli."

"What a lovely place!"

"What a lovely place," Harley agreed. "We register over there?"

"Yes, sir. Can I help with the bags?"

"I've got 'em."

Harley grunted onward, and the bellhop melted back into the yakking throng.

"Why didn't you let him help with the bags?"

"Did you see how skinny that kid was? He couldn't carry these bags."

"He could get a cart."

"He could pick up the bags, then I could carry *him* under my arm. How would that be?"

"You just don't want to tip him."

Harley sighed. "I've got the bags."

"All right, big guy. I'll follow you."

While he lugged luggage, I trailed behind, eavesdropping. I didn't recognize anyone famous, but the talk definitely was about the film festival.

"Did you hear about that documentary from Ethiopia?" asked an older woman with Bozo-red hair. "Absolutely heartbreaking. All that starvation and degradation."

"I heard," said her buxom friend. "I can't wait to see it!"

A young man (whose own hair appeared to have survived some sort of electrical accident) was complaining about the festival's judging, which apparently had kept his entry out of the program. He was being vigorously ignored by a Goth girl who had a ring through her nose like a prize bull.

"I hear Spielberg's got a scout here," a man in a fedora said to a lady in a turban. "This could be the new place to get discovered."

"The way Sundance *used* to be," she sighed.

Two men stood apart from the others, and I noticed them because they didn't seem to belong together. One was all sharp angles and high energy as he talked rapidly into a tiny phone. He wore hipster eyeglasses and creased jeans and two-toned shoes. The other guy was round and half-asleep and perhaps homeless, dressed in a frayed blue baseball cap and an Eraserhead T-shirt that had been washed about a thousand times. He had the kind of bushy beard that makes you think of cooties.

I was wearing regular clothes --- black slacks and a fitted red sweater and flats -- and Harley was dressed in jeans and boots like any other small-town New Mexican, but in this crowd, I felt like *we* were the ones who stood out. I'll bet none of these tattooed weirdos insisted on carrying their own bags.

They all busily thumbed their cell phones while carrying on full-fledged live conversations, and I wondered how they could keep it all straight. Maybe they were all texting each other about the yokels in their midst.

You don't see such multi-tasking in Pandora. Life's slower there, so we mostly do only one thing at a time. If you need to get information to people, you usually can wait until you run into them at the supermarket. Hell, you can tell something to a loudmouth like Mitzi Tyner, and within hours the whole town will know--

"Loretta!"

"Huh? What?"

Harley appeared annoyed. "I said, 'Is the reservation under your name?'"

"Oh. I don't remember, Harley. Probably."

He managed not to roll his eyes (I can always tell) as he turned back to the plump desk clerk. She pounded on her keyboard some more as he spelled my name for her.

"Ah," she said. "There it is."

Harley whewed and got out his credit card and secured our lodging. I turned to gawk some more, and saw a familiar face.

"Hilda!"

She was edging through the babbling horde, her leather bag clutched to her narrow chest.

"Hilda! Over here! It's Loretta!"

She heard me this time, and smiled when she spotted me standing next to Harley and our heap of luggage.

Hilda Schmidt always seemed harried and overwhelmed. She'd worked for Michael Girard nearly three years now, longer than his personal assistants usually last. Not that Mr. Girard isn't a dream to work with, everyone says so, but it's an around-the-

clock job. His assistants tend to be young women like Hilda --
slender, nervous greyhounds who run really fast until they burn
out. I hoped Hilda wasn't nearing that point because I enjoyed
working with her.

Whenever I need anything from Mr. Girard for the fan
club, Hilda's the one I contact. Most of our interaction is by e-
mail (she's always very polite and uses full sentences,
punctuated perfectly), but maybe twice a month we talk on the
phone, setting up a contest or getting some last-minute info onto
the website, and it's during these conversations that we've really
gotten to know each other. I've heard all about her childhood in
the Midwest and her tiny apartment in Culver City and her bad
luck with a string of shiftless boyfriends. We've met in person
twice -- at a fan club convention in Phoenix and again when
Harley and I went to L.A. on vacation -- and I've found her to
be very down-to-earth, if a little tightly wound. She seemed
even more uptight than usual as I gave her a big hug.

I introduced Harley, and he said all the right things.

Hilda's got stick-straight brown hair and she's bony all
over, but she was dressed nicely in slacks and a silk blouse and
dangly earrings. She seemed distracted, but, Lord love a duck,
imagine how much she must've had on her plate, what with Mr.
Girard being the guest of honor and all.

My breath caught in my throat. If Hilda was here
already, that most likely meant Michael Girard was nearby.

"Is he here?" I blurted, talking over whatever Harley had been going on about. Farm machinery or something.

Hilda smiled. "He's upstairs. Getting a little nap before the big night."

I tingled all the way to my toes. Michael Girard was in this very building this very minute. Oh, my.

"Loretta? Are you all right?"

"What do you mean, Harley?"

"You're all red in the face. Are you having a hot flash?"

"*No*, I'm not," I said. "Much too young for hot flashes. But thanks for asking, *sweetheart*."

"Oops." Harley grinned at Hilda. "Made her mad. Again."

I plastered a big smile on my face. The kind that looks plastered on. "It does seem a little warm in here."

Hilda glanced over her shoulder at the yammering herd. "Lot of hot air."

Harley har-harred at that, louder than necessary, trying to make nice. I slipped Hilda a wink and changed the subject.

"We all set for our big interview tomorrow?"

"I think so," she said. "Everything's been a little *fluid* since we got here, if you know what I mean."

"I have no idea what that means."

She spoke just above a whisper. Harley and I both leaned in, and it's a wonder we didn't all crack skulls.

"The film festival seems a little disorganized," she said. "It's the first time they've put it together, you know? Have to expect things to be ragged."

Harley said, "Any way we can help?"

(See why I love this man? He's just met this young woman. He certainly has no reason to help out Michael Girard, who has, after all, been a lifelong distraction for me. Yet, when he hears there's a problem, his first inclination is to jump right in, offering to help. He's always been that way.)

"No, no," she said. "Everything's okay. But don't expect anything to run on schedule this weekend."

Harley started gathering up our bags, but I wasn't finished talking to Hilda. I was opening my mouth to tell him to go up to the room without me when a man barged into our little group.

"Miss Schmidt? Hilda?"

It was the angular man I'd noticed a few minutes earlier, the one with the narrow eyeglasses and the cell phone. His hairy friend with the baseball cap trailed behind him.

"I thought that was you!" The hipster thrust out his hand for her to shake. "Kip Kaplin! The producer? We talked on the phone the other day?"

Hilda stiffened all over, but managed to keep a pleasant smile on her face.

"Oh, yes. Mr. Kaplin. We've spoken many times."

"Right! Haha! That's me. Always on the phone."

He held up his little phone, as if in evidence. It looked very high-tech and well-worn. When Hilda didn't respond, he dragged the bearded guy up to shake paws with her, too.

"This is the director I told you about on the phone," Kaplin said. "Sean Hyde, meet Hilda Schmidt."

"Oh, right," she said. "You directed 'Paranoid Fits' and 'Laugh of the Zombie.'"

He mumbled something into his thick beard, and might've even blushed, but it was hard to tell because he was such a ball of hair.

"And now you want to direct a *Western*?"

"That's what we'd like to talk to you about," Kaplin said quickly. "If we could get a meeting with you and Mr. Girard while we're all here. Drinks, whatever."

"I don't know," Hilda said. "Our schedule's full up."

"There must be a little air in there," Kaplin said brightly. "A little down time or something. You guys are staying in the penthouse, right? We are, too! So, we're, like, right down the hall and happy to get together whenever it's convenient."

"Well, maybe--"

"Hey, if Mr. Girard's at all interested, we can drive him out to Gray Ranch, where we'd do a lot of the filming. It's this complete Old West town where they filmed 'Silverado.'"

"I'm sure we won't have time for that," Hilda said, flushing. "Mr. Girard has to be back in L.A. first thing Monday morning."

Harley and I still stood there like a couple of cigar-store Indians, and Hilda used us as a diversion, introducing us and making a big deal out of the fact that I was the president of the International Michael Girard Fan Club. She made it sound like an honored position, but I could see the others' eyes glaze over. I was just a fan, I couldn't do them any good, so I was invisible.

Harley resumed gathering up our bags. Hilda looked at me with pleading in her eyes, but she needn't worry. I had no intention of abandoning her to these two slickers.

"Hilda? We need to dump our stuff upstairs. You want to come with us?"

Harley, arms full of luggage, gave me a look.

"Oh, no, Loretta, but thank you. I've got to get some papers copied and run them over to the theater. I'm already late."

She made a show of looking at her wrist, which bore no watch. We bid our farewells and let her scurry away.

Harley insisted on carrying all the bags, so I pushed the elevator button and smiled at passers-by until we were alone in an elevator.

"Could you believe those guys?" I said. "What a couple of weirdos. I thought they were going to grab Hilda and wrestle her to the ground and make her listen to their stupid movie idea."

"Must be lots of grubby guys like them at film festivals," Harley said. "Every time Mr. Girard makes an appearance, there'll be a stampede of people waving scripts at him."

"Oh, God. I'm going to seem like just another clingy grubber, wasting Mr. Girard's time with my interview."

"Not at all, Loretta. Unlike those jerks, you don't *want* anything except a little bit of his time. He gets a big benefit year-round from the fan club. I'm sure he'll be delighted to see you."

"I just want to make a good impression."

He grinned. "After all these Hollywood phonies, you're gonna seem like a breath of fresh air."

Chapter 5

After we freshened up, Harley and I decided to walk to the Zia Theater, where we'd get our official film festival registration packets. It wasn't far to the theater, which was just as well, because who knew whether we'd ever get our Suburban back? That valet was probably halfway to Las Vegas.

Harley did not seem to appreciate these observations as we strolled the covered sidewalks, dodging wooden posts and gawking tourists. The shop windows were filled with delights -- Navajo rugs, beautiful jewelry, fabulous artwork and antiques. I could've spent all day in those stores, but not Harley. He bulled down the sidewalk as if he were blocking for me. By the time we reached the theater, I felt I should throw down a football and do a little touchdown dance. Another observation that seemed to go right over his head.

(Harley approaches any trip the same way he approaches his work or a chore at home: Determined to get from point A to point B in the most efficient manner and with the fewest distractions. He might as well be wearing blinders. And earmuffs.)

Above the entrance of the Zia Theater towered an old-fashioned neon-edged marquee, which currently read: "Welcome to the 1st annual SFSSSFF!"

"They need to change the name of this festival," I told Harley. "That's never going to catch on."

"Maybe if they put it in giant orange letters," he suggested. "Like KIMBALLS."

We got a chuckle out of that, and were all smiles as we reached the theater entrance. A milling crowd outside the door was similar to the one we'd seen in the hotel lobby -- a mix of urban cool and Hollywood casual and New Mexico homespun. They didn't seem to be in line or anything. Harley plunged through them and I swam along in his wake, smiling at the people he nearly bowled over.

The lobby was gorgeous, with high ceilings and plaster walls and arched doorways. The zia symbol repeated in the tilework, along with other geometrics that hinted at Native American origin. The ceiling and walls featured huge murals showing Indian dancers in a landscape of redrock ridges and clear blue skies. The dancers were dressed as bison and eagles and deer, their costumes intricately detailed. I was so busy gawking at the paintings that I nearly walked up Harley's back when he stopped abruptly in front of the registration table.

The smiling volunteers behind the table seemed slightly confused, as if all the envelopes and files and badges had been set up by someone else who'd left them no instructions. I've seen sock drawers that were better organized. Reminded me of every PTA bake sale in the history of Pandora. I've often said we'd be better off having a charity pie fight every year. The preparation and clean-up couldn't be any worse than it is now, and people don't need all those calories anyway--

"Loretta!"

"Yes, Harley?"

"They need to see your credit card since you're the one who reserved the tickets."

He seemed a little flustered, but I didn't mind breaking out my credit card. It was about to burn a hole in my pocketbook anyway.

A volunteer looked at the card through her bifocals, then checked her paperwork and cleared us for takeoff. The other ladies loaded us up with badges and tickets and souvenir programs and tote bags full of swag. I could hardly wait to get back to our room and sift through the goodies, but I could tell Harley's blood sugar was dipping, and he would get cranky if I didn't get some food in him soon.

"Hon, you want to find a coffee? Maybe a snack?"

"Huh?"

He was looking through an envelope that contained tickets to various events. His brow was so knit in concentration, it was in danger of becoming a sweater.

"You need to relax, Harley. Let's get you an ice cream or something. You've been going so hard, doing all the driving and toting and stuff, you must be exhausted."

He nodded and stuffed the envelope in his tote bag. This time, I led the way through the lobby.

As we reached the exit, a man burst through the door, sobbing, and practically fell into my arms. He was my height and thin, but seemed more imposing because of the sweeping velvet cape draped around his shoulders. The black cape matched the streaks on his face where his mascara was running.

"This is awful!" he bawled. "Awful! I cannot go on!"

He looked back over his shoulder at a plump bald man and a young woman who came chasing through the door after him. She was one of those naturally beautiful Hispanic girls, slender and dark, with tawny skin and doe eyes and curly black hair that fell to her shoulders. The egg-shaped guy was dressed in white shirt and white pants, as if he were a paramedic or a Good Humor man. He held his arms out to embrace the bawler, who was having none of it.

"Stay back, Tony! I do not wish to be comforted!"

Tony's fleshy face sagged, and he let his arms fall to his sides. The woman rolled her eyes.

"Come on, Andre," she said. "This doesn't rate such a meltdown."

Andre sniffed and pulled himself up to his full height, which I could now see was enhanced by flamenco boots with two-inch heels. He also wore a black silk shirt and tight black pants. The Zorro look.

"This is *not* a 'meltdown,'" he said haughtily. "This is genuine emotion. You cannot imagine the stress that I'm under."

"I've got some idea," she said.

"No, you do not. This festival is bigger than anything you've masterminded in your young life. All we've asked of the film commission is a little cooperation, a little *support*."

They were so busy bickering, nobody had thought to offer the poor man a hanky. I pulled some fresh Kleenex from my purse and pressed it into his hand. He thanked me as he dabbed away black tears.

"I nearly crashed right into you," he said.

He looked us up and down, and his eyes settled on the film festival tote bags in our hands.

"Please accept my apologies." He held out a limp, damp hand for us to shake. "My name is Andre de Carlo."

He paused, giving us time to recognize him as someone famous. When we both just stood there gaping, he added, "Director of the film festival."

We introduced ourselves, and Harley asked, "Has something gone wrong?"

Andre gave his head a shake as he struggled to retain his composure. His hair was slightly shaggy, dyed the sort of matte black you get when you try to hide the gray.

"I'm just overwrought," he said. "So many details! I thought I could count on *some people* to help."

He aimed this last comment at the young woman, who sighed wearily. I finally noticed the name badge pinned to her blue blazer. It said, "Maria Mondragon, New Mexico Film Commission."

The film commission hands out tax breaks and other incentives to lure filmmakers to our state, and it's a real success story. They make so many movies and shows here these days, you can hardly turn on a TV without seeing our sweeping landscapes and turquoise skies.

Tony tried again to hug Andre, who this time allowed the embrace. If Andre hadn't been wearing the heels, the two would've been the same height, but Tony was twice as wide. He patted Andre's back and kissed him on both cheeks.

"Okay, Tony. That's enough. Thank you, dear. I'll be all right in a moment."

We don't have a lot of gays in Pandora. I mean, I'm sure we have the same percentage of gays that you find anyplace, but not many who live an "out" lifestyle. Certainly, you never see men kissing there. But these two smooched completely unselfconsciously. I thought it was kind of cute.

Harley cleared his throat, but I didn't look over at him. I wanted to meet Maria Mondragon. I could use a source at the film commission as I round up news for the fan club website. I squeezed past the two boyfriends, and offered her my hand.

"So nice to meet you," I said. "Harley and I are both native New Mexicans, and think you all do great work at the film commission. Isn't that right, Harley?"

He nodded, but couldn't seem to find any words. Too goggle-eyed over the kissing men.

I told her we were from Pandora and that I was president of the International Michael Girard Fan Club, which didn't get much of a rise out of her. Her dark eyes kept cutting over to Andre, as if she weren't done with him.

"Have you been with the film commission long?"

"No, I'm new."

"She's an *intern*!" Andre screeched. "*That's* what they think of our film festival. *That's* what we're worth to them!"

He buried his head in Tony's meaty shoulder and boohooed some more. Tony made "sorry" eyes at Maria, who tossed her curly mane.

(I should go on record right here and say that, despite the drama of this first encounter, I took an immediate liking to Maria Mondragon. I'm frankly prejudiced toward people who have curly, unruly hair like mine. I know that each morning is a trial for them.)

"I am an intern," she said tightly, "but it's supposed to turn into a full-time position as soon as the Legislature approves the new state budget."

"Congratulations!" I meant it, but she must've thought I was joshing because she rolled her eyes in that elaborate way of today's youth.

"They assigned me to be liaison to this film festival because I was the only one in the office not booked up to the eyeballs. We've already got film festivals all over New Mexico, and every one wants a liaison with the film commission. So does every location scout and director and fly-by-night producer who might, someday, maybe, shoot something here. They all want a personal pipeline to tax dollars and publicity and VIP treatment, and what they get instead is somebody like me."

She glared at Andre, daring him to speak. He and Tony shrank back wide-eyed, clutching each other.

Maria stomped out of the lobby and disappeared around the corner. We could hear her heels clacking on the brick sidewalk long after we could no longer see her.

"Good lord," said Andre with a sniff. "What a drama queen!"

Chapter 6

Harley and I stopped in an ice cream shop and purchased him a chocolate-dipped vanilla cone (for the price of a full meal at the Cozy Nook Diner back home). The listless soda jerk took forever, even though we were the only customers in the place.

The temperature outside was dropping, along with the sun, but the ice cream still was melting all over Harley's hand as we entered the lobby of the Hotel Kokopelli. My mothering instincts made me want to clean him up, but I'd given away all my Kleenex.

I was so busy fretting over Harley's stickiness that we were well inside before I realized the dynamic in the lobby had changed. The hipsters and cowpunks no longer clustered in pairs and trios. They were gathered into a mob near the spouting Kokopelli fountain, gazing admiringly at a woman who was the center of attention.

Mitzi Tyner.

"Oh, for shit's sake," Harley said. "Would you look at that?"

How could I look at anything else? There stood my arch-nemesis, completely at home among these strangers. Her unnaturally black hair was perfectly coiffed and her smile was so white that it made her teeth look fake. (They're not, but they've had a lot of help.) As reported by the gossips of Pandora, she'd gone nuts for Santa Fe style: Squash-blossom necklace, cowgirl boots, a long denim skirt embroidered with cactus flowers. To top it off, she wore a fuzzy black-and-white vest that appeared to be made from the hide of a deceased Shetland pony.

Next to Mitzi, Nannette Hoch looked like a "before" photo. With her loose gray dress and artlessly tousled hair, Nannette appeared to have rolled out of bed and landed in a feed sack. She stared adoringly at her friend, and it encouraged the others to do the same.

Mitzi spotted us across the lobby and started yoo-hooing and calling my name, and I had no choice but to wave back if I wanted to shut her up.

"I'll go over and say hello."

"Loretta." Harley's voice had an edge of warning in it.

"It's okay. Go to that men's room over there and wash up. I'll meet you at the elevators."

He hesitated. "You sure?"

"Might as well get it over with."

Soon as Mitzi saw I was doing her bidding, she resumed addressing the assembled, finishing whatever ribald joke or lame anecdote had them so enthralled. She got a burst of admiring laughter just as I joined them, and it made me want to go through the crowd, pinching each and every one. Instead, I glued on a smile as big as Mitzi's own.

"Loretta!" she exclaimed, as if seeing me for the first time all over again. "Come meet my new friends. Everyone, this is Loretta. She's from Pandora, too."

Great. Already, I'm "that other woman" from Pandora. Her admirers looked me over, but didn't find anything to fascinate them, and went back to hanging on Mitzi's every word.

"Loretta is president of the International Michael Girard Fan Club." Mitzi made her eyes go round, which must've taken quite an effort considering how much mascara weighed down her eyelashes. "Isn't that a hoot?"

They all laughed and nodded. (Except for Nannette, who glowered at me, as usual.)

Being fan club president most certainly is not a "hoot." It's a responsibility I take most seriously, and it's a ton of work, not that Mitzi would have any idea what that means.

"Speaking of hoots," I said, looking her up and down, "did you run off and join the rodeo?"

A hush fell over Mitzi's mob and malicious grins lit up their faces. Nothing they'd like more than a catfight.

Mitzi propped up her perpetual smile. "Just getting into the spirit of the event, dear. You should try it sometime."

Oh, of all the nerve. After *I* was the one who had to wear the stupid bumblebee costume when the Busy Bee Homemakers Club visited the shut-ins. If that's not getting in the spirit of an event, I don't know what is. Of course, none of the film festival snoots knew or cared about the truth. They preferred to believe we Westerners go around dressed as Annie Oakley, saying things like "hoot."

"Haven't had time to think about such things," I said. "I've been swamped ever since we arrived."

"Really? Doing what?"

"Oh, I had to meet with Michael Girard's assistant about my interview with him. And I just came from a meeting with the festival organizers and a nice young woman from the state film commission."

You know how flowers turn their heads in unison to find the rays of the sun? That's exactly what the hipsters looked like, turning away from Mitzi and toward me. I'd emitted the Hollywood version of sunshine -- connections -- and suddenly had their undivided attention.

Tough luck for them. I had no intention of saying more, so they could dissect my tenuous links to the aforementioned big shots or the accidental nature of my "meetings." I'd scored my little victory, and I was getting out while the getting was good.

"Oh, look. There's Harley. Gotta run!"

I gave the disappointed crowd a smile and breezed away amid a chorus of "awwws." A couple of scuzzy young guys who looked like they made documentaries followed in my wake, business cards in hand, but they faded when they saw Harley holding the elevator door for me.

I gave the crowd a little wave as the doors closed, but I only had eyes for Mitzi. Behind her frozen smile, she was deeply pissed off, which made me happy in ways I cannot describe.

After the doors closed, Harley said, "What the heck happened out there?"

"Oh, nothing," I said smugly. "Just a little mingling."

"You must be a damn good mingler."

"I have my moments."

FAN FAIR: THE OFFICIAL WEBSITE OF THE
INTERNATIONAL MICHAEL GIRARD FAN CLUB
5:32 p.m. March 24

From the President:

Greetings from Santa Fe! I've got just a minute to give the briefest of updates, then I must get gussied up for tonight's big gala, where we'll see Mr. Girard in person!

It's been quite an eventful day, and the festival's not even officially under way yet. Upon arrival, my husband and I picked up our registration materials for the Santa Fe Silver Screen Society Film Festival, and we each were given a bag full of neat stuff from Hollywood: buttons and ballpoints and refrigerator magnets and T-shirts, all advertising various films that'll be shown here. Quite the haul!

The Hotel Kokopelli is lovely, though the rooms are a tad on the small side and the minibar apparently holds the most valuable snack items in the world. Great location, though. Only three blocks from the plaza.

Much of the fun at a film festival is the gabbing and networking that goes on, and we've already witnessed plenty. Everyone here seems to have a project to "pitch" to anyone who will listen. Mostly, they just talk to each other to keep their dreams alive.

I haven't recognized any movie stars yet, but I'm sure there will be plenty on the red carpet at tonight's gala!

Another update, with more details, soon.

Sincerely,

Loretta Kimball, president, IMGFC

Chapter 7

Okay, there wasn't a red carpet. Not as such. But they did have red velvet ropes on stanchions to funnel new arrivals to the correct doors. Tourists and fangirls pressed against the ropes with their cameras and autograph books, and that made it feel like arriving at the Oscars.

Sleek stretch limos pulled up outside the theater and dumped their loads, one after another. Harley and I had to wait for a break in the traffic to cross the street, and I leaned on him to take some of the weight off my feet, which already ached in my three-inch heels.

Despite a chilly breeze ruffling our hair, Harley and I looked pretty special as we arrived, and a few people snapped our photograph before they realized we weren't famous. Harley's bowtie was crooked, but he still looked good in his tux. I was beaming, of course. My long green gown and pinching shoes required me to take tiny steps, so it might've appeared that I was milking the moment, which wasn't the case at all, but I do admit I enjoyed the limelight.

Then we entered the lobby, where hundreds of revelers were packed together like well-dressed sardines. Everybody talked at once, and we were hit by a wave of noise and hot air that made it difficult to keep smiling. Harley's glasses steamed up, so he was stone blind. I already had hold of his elbow from the promenade into the theater, and I tugged him to a stop before he could collide with somebody important.

Talk about sensory overload. So much noise and color! So many glamorous and/or strange people packed into one space! Such fashion choices! Bouffant hairdos and sparkly gowns and frankly odd hats and unsightly face jewelry.

(I do not understand why today's youth insist on poking holes in themselves. It simply is not attractive. But that's a sermon for another day.)

Lots of skin on display for late March, but what the hell, maybe the young women had the right idea. It was about eighty-five degrees in the lobby, and all the oxygen had been used up an hour ago.

Harley could see none of this, of course, as he wiped his glasses on his cummerbund. Fortunately, in my painful stilettos, I was as tall as him and could serve as lookout. I didn't want Mitzi and Nannette to glom onto us. I would not let them ruin this night.

Beside me stood a scarlet-lipped young woman wearing a dress that appeared to be made entirely of spirals of gray movie film. How she held it up, I don't know. No visible means of support. I could've yanked one dangling end, and she would've spun like a top until naked.

She was chatting with a middle-aged man who wore a thigh-length black sweater, knee-high athletic socks and sneakers. No visible pants. Oh, my.

Quickly turning away, I found two tiny Hispanic men dressed in what appeared to be glittery matador costumes, sans hats and capes. I hoped they were part of the night's entertainment. But this was Santa Fe. Maybe they dressed like that every day.

Beyond them stood a couple of thirty-year-old urbanites with black clothes and carefully bored expressions. The woman's ears were pierced with what appeared to be cup hooks, and it made me wonder whether she worked in a coffee shop. They were trying to ignore the two turquoise-drenched snowbirds next to them, who were shouting into each other's hearing aids about whether they'd taken their pills before they left the house.

A woman with frizzy yellow hair and unnaturally large eyes pressed up against Harley, a goofy grin on her face. It was like being assaulted by Big Bird. But it wasn't as if she could help crowding him. The bearded man on the other side of her was built like steamroller. Just looking at him made me want to sweat.

"I'm the only one wearing a tuxedo," Harley said glumly.

"Oh, that's not true. There's one right over there!"

"I think that's an usher."

Looking around, I could see he was more or less right. Most of the men looked downright scruffy. Unshaven and unwashed, with their shirttails hanging out and holes in their jeans. Trying for that casual disdain so popular among the younger Hollywood stars. Or maybe just too drunk and/or doped up to figure out their shirt buttons.

To me, it shows respect for the event to dress appropriately. As my late mother always said, you can't really *over*dress for a party, but you sure as heck can embarrass yourself by *under*dressing. This crowd proved Mother right.

Harley had noticed that some of the ingénues were damned near naked, and he was sneaking peeks right and left until he saw me watching, then he got real interested in the ceiling murals.

The minutes ticked past. People around us checked their watches and muttered. Isn't it time for the gala to begin? Shouldn't we be allowed into the (hopefully, cooler) theater so we can find our seats? What the heck's going on? The muttering spread across the lobby and reached mutinous levels before finally being interrupted by a shrieking whistle.

The hubbub died. All heads swiveled toward the source of that piercing sound.

Andre de Carlo stood on a chair behind the concession stand counter, his pinky fingers still wedged in the corners of his mouth. He cocked a penciled eyebrow, as if daring us to ask for another. When no one made a peep, he removed his fingers and shouted, "Thank you for your attention!"

This caused the noise to start right up again. Andre rolled his eyes heavenward, though he'd dressed wrong for that direction. He still wore tight black clothes, but now his cape was red satin. All he needed to complete the look were horns and a pitchfork.

"People!" he shouted. "People! So sorry for the delay! We had a last-minute conflict with the fire marshal, but it's all worked out now, and we'll open the doors shortly."

This was met with a murmur of approval. Encouraged, Andre added, "The show must go on!"

He looked disappointed at the pitiful spattering of applause, but we were all wedged so tightly together that few of us could move our arms. Andre allowed his boyfriend to help him down off the chair. Plump Tony wore a white shirt, brown pants and a pink cummerbund.

"I've got a sudden craving for Neapolitan ice cream," I said to Harley, but he didn't get it. Too busy trying to edge away from Big Bird. I wished he would stop crowding me. I was trying not to crunch up against the young woman dressed in old movies. I'd lost sight of her pants-free friend, but before I could worry about that, the theater doors opened and the crowd surged forward in a slow-motion stampede.

Steamroller Man blocked all progress through our door for a moment -- the cork in the bottleneck -- but soon we plunged into the cool, dim airiness of the beautiful old theater. Once inside, Harley and I moved out of the traffic flow and stood together, taking deep breaths.

The high ceiling was decorated with more murals of Pueblo dancers, and the chandeliers and wall sconces were shaped like arrowheads. The seats were dark maroon, as were the proscenium curtains and the patterned carpet.

"Better in here," Harley gasped.

"Yes, but we shouldn't stand around. We should get to our seats before Mitzi finds us."

"Right."

We located our seats, which were only four rows from the stage, if a little off to one side. Harley paused to hitch his britches and look around the place, and I grabbed his sleeve and yanked him down into his chair.

"Mitzi will see you!"

"What's she gonna do, Loretta? It's not like she can join us. They're assigned seats."

"She might come over and talk to us."

"Oh, yeah, that would be terrible. We'd have to kill ourselves then."

I chose to ignore that remark. I looked all around the audience as best I could while slumping low in my chair. The white-haired couple next to me seemed a little alarmed by my secretive manner. I gave them my best winning smile, but it didn't help.

No sign of Mitzi. I did see those two movie guys -- Kip Kaplin and Sean Hyde -- across the way. Kaplin was talking on a cell phone while the hairy director stared vacantly at the empty stage. I guessed that the other folks I knew -- Hilda Schmidt and the festival organizers and Maria Mondragon and Mr. Girard -- were all backstage. I ached to be back there among them, a fly on the wall, but I didn't let on to Harley. Instead, I took his big hand in both of mine.

"Thank you, Harley."

"For what?"

"All this. You made it possible. For me. For us."

He tried to cover his blush by pushing up his smudged glasses.

"Love you, big guy."

"I love you, too, Loretta."

The house lights flickered, but it was an irregular heartbeat, no rhythm to its intent. Then the auditorium went completely dark, as black as Mitzi Tyner's heart. The audience gasped, then hushed, everyone waiting for illumination.

Out of this silence came an abrupt scream, a woman's voice spiraling in terror. It was enough to curl your toenails.

The lights flashed back to life. The crowd buzzed, heads whipping around as we sought the source of the shriek.

A young couple stood frozen in the center aisle, and from the crimson glow of her face, it was clear the dark-haired girl was the screamer. Her boyfriend was blushing, too. Nervous laughter rippled across the theater, then everyone was talking at once, most making the same assumption Harley did: "I'll bet that boy goosed her in the dark."

"He goosed her somewhere," I said.

The couple, still brightly embarrassed, found their row and edged toward their seats.

Harley peeled my fingernails out of the back of his hand and said, "Are you okay?"

"I'm fine. Why do you ask?"

"You seem a little jumpy."

"I'm just excited. I wish they'd turn the house lights out again. Mitzi's here somewhere."

"Stop thinking about Mitzi. Enjoy yourself."

The lights went down slowly this time, and the crowd noise fell away. Footlights illuminated the edge of the stage, then Andre de Carlo swept into view under the glare of a spotlight. The audience applauded madly as Andre swirled his red cape and bowed deeply.

"Thank you, thank you," he said into a cordless microphone, which responded with a spurt of squealing feedback. Andre winced and held the microphone at arm's length.

"Good evening, and welcome to the first annual film festival produced by the Santa Fe Silver Screen Society!"

We all clapped like crazy, and Andre bowed some more. (Milking it a little, if you ask me.)

"I am festival director Andre de Carlo, and I hope you all have a wonderful time, discovering new films and learning more about the stars of yesteryear."

More applause, but mine was less enthusiastic. I didn't like the implication that Mr. Girard might be part of "yesteryear." His career is still quite vibrant, thank you, and he's done some of his most challenging work recently, in small independent films such as "Pound of Flesh" and "Snickerdoodle." But never mind.

Andre gave a brief speech about how he came up with the idea for the event (as if no one had ever thought of a film festival before), and he thanked all the volunteers who made it possible.

"And, finally," he sighed, "I must thank the love of my life, who has stood by me through all the emotional upheaval that comes with planning an event like this. My port in the storm: Tony Lodge!"

He pointed stage right, but it was dark over there, and we could barely see Tony as he stepped out onto the stage, waving. The spotlight operator swung Andre's spot over to find Tony, then left him again to return to Andre, who remained at center stage, one hand on his hip, a picture of pique.

"I apologize for the lighting difficulties," he said. "It's so hard to get good help these days."

The follow spot moved six feet to the left and stayed there, illuminating empty stage. Titters ran around the room like mice. After a tense few seconds, Andre walked into the spotlight, displaying a clenched smile.

"That's show business," he said. "Everyone wants to get in on the act."

That got a nice laugh, and the room seemed to relax. But not me. I'd gone on full alert. I'd spotted Mitzi, not thirty feet away, parading down the aisle toward the stage, Nannette trailing behind her like a shadow.

I felt Harley's restraining hand on my arm, but I couldn't take my eyes off Mitzi.

She took her time reaching her front-row seat so we could all get a good look at her new outfit. She wore the flat-topped hat the gossips in Pandora had warned me about, along with a sparkly little jacket and a flowing skirt that was done in swirling reds and oranges and yellows, so it looked like she was standing in a fire.

Even Andre seemed to be staring at Mitzi, despite the footlights glaring in his eyes, but she showed no embarrassment over interrupting his welcoming remarks.

"Oh, the *nerve* of that woman!"

Harley shushed me, though I had spoken in a restrained whisper. People around us turned to stare, but I ignored them, too busy trying to set Mitzi's hat ablaze with the intensity of my glare. (It didn't work. It never does.)

Nannette wore the same mouse-gray dress she'd worn in the afternoon, and she was practically invisible as she slipped into the seat next to Mitzi.

Once they were settled, Andre snapped out of it and wrapped up his thank-yous.

"And now." He paused dramatically, as if waiting for a drumroll. "It's time to meet some of the *stars* who are participating in the festival!"

More applause. Finally, what we'd all come to see.

"First and foremost, the person who really has made this all possible -- Ava Andrews!"

The actress floated onto the stage in a white gown decorated in dazzling crystal beadwork. Her still-blond hair was done up in a French twist, and she wore dangling earrings that glinted as she joined Andre in the spotlight.

She didn't look much older than when she starred years ago as Maggie Greenhalt, the matriarch on "Empire," a role that won her an Emmy for best actress. She looked so good, in fact, that I speculated that she'd had a lot of "work" done, though I would never say anything so tacky out loud.

She gave Andre a quick hug, then took the microphone from him. It protested with a squeal of feedback, but Ava scarcely seemed to notice as she thanked us all for coming and thanked Andre for putting the festival together and blah, blah, like that.

I was distracted because Mitzi had produced an ornate paper fan from somewhere upon her person and snapped it open. She flapped it at her face, like a moth in the footlights. It wasn't even that warm in the theater! But, oh, Mitzi couldn't *stand* it that someone else might be the center of attention.

Ava Andrews didn't appear to notice the fluttering at her feet. She started naming "dear friends" who were in attendance. We all swiveled in our chairs, trying to get glimpses of the bloated has-beens and up-and-coming starlets and obscure directors who briefly stood when their names were called. By the time she'd reeled off a dozen such acknowledgments, the applause was clamorous. Up on the stage, Andre de Carlo pounded his tiny hands together so enthusiastically, you might've thought they were on fire and he was trying to put them out.

Ava beamed while she waited for the applause to die.

"And now," she said, "I'd like to introduce a special friend of mine. My co-star on 'Empire' and a real gentleman in every way--"

Oh, how my heart raced!

"Ladies and gentleman, Roger Sherwood!"

Ooh, that burned me up. How dare Roger Sherwood (that rat) show up at this event when everyone knows he *stole* the role of Charles Greenhalt right out from under Mr. Girard after the second season of "Empire."

He strolled onto the stage like he belonged there, smiling and waving. He wore a gray suit over a black T-shirt, as if doing a cameo on "Miami Vice." Way too casual, if you ask me. If he must show up here, trying to steal Mr. Girard's thunder, he could at least put on a necktie.

Some people will applaud for anything, and I suppose Roger Sherwood (that rat) is considered by some to be a big star. At least he didn't try to give a speech. He simply waved and disappeared back into the wings.

"Roger will be gracing us with more appearances throughout the festival," Ava Andrews warned. "But now it's time to meet our guest of honor. A dear friend and a truly great actor: Michael Girard!"

Mr. Girard strode onto the stage, smiling graciously. His posture was ramrod straight, as always, and his silvery hair glinted. He looked tanned and fit, and he had a twinkle in his famous blue eyes.

The crowd rose in a standing ovation. I might've been the first one on her feet.

"Look," Harley shouted over the applause, "he's wearing a tuxedo!"

"Of course he is," I said, but I don't know if Harley heard me. I couldn't take my eyes off Mr. Girard. He's got that kind of presence. The crowd noise seemed to drop away, and the periphery of my vision blurred until it was as if I were staring through a long tunnel and Mr. Girard stood at the far end. It felt as if the temperature in the theater rose thirty degrees during the ovation.

Ava Andrews must've been wearing high heels under her gown because she and Mr. Girard were nearly the same height as they air-kissed up on stage. She beamed at him, and who could blame her? He evokes that sort of response from people. They're just happy to be near him.

She gave Mr. Girard the cordless mike, and he thanked us all for "that heart-warming welcome."

Harley tugged on my elbow, and I snapped out of it and realized that everyone else had stopped clapping and returned to their seats. I dropped into my chair, embarrassed, but nobody was paying attention to me. The audience was transfixed by Mr. Girard.

"When I first received the invitation to this film festival," he said, "I was flattered, of course, but also surprised. Santa Fe? I'd never been to Santa Fe before, if you can believe that."

A chuckle skittered through the audience.

"What a delightful city! I've been a bug-eyed tourist since I arrived. Can't wait to look around some more."

Oh, we all loved that, of course. Hometown crowd, etc. He waited out the applause, smiling bemusedly.

"I thank the Santa Fe Silver Screen Society for selecting me as guest of honor."

Another round of applause. Andre tossed his red cape at the mention of his organization. Made me glad there weren't any bulls nearby.

"This festival is extra-special to me, of course, because Ava Andrews is able to be here."

Mr. Girard reached out, and they clasped hands and looked into each other's eyes with the same sort of affection so apparent on the first two seasons of "Empire," before the contract dispute that resulted in Mr. Girard being replaced. These two genuinely liked and respected each other. You could just tell.

"When Ava first approached me about this event, I insisted on one thing: That time be built into the festival schedule for me to really interact with the folks who are attending."

That got an even bigger round of applause, as you might expect, but Mr. Girard waved it down so he could finish.

"Starting tonight, I hope to meet each and every one of you in person. I look forward to it!"

Another standing ovation. I jumped up so quickly, I nearly fell off my tall shoes. Harley steadied me, but I barely noticed. I was too busy slapping my palms together like an excited chimp. The stars waved their way off the stage amid an enormous round of applause. By the time we were done clapping, I was exhausted.

After everyone quieted, Andre suffered through another round of shrieking feedback (some people are simply unlucky with electronics), then announced that refreshments would be served in the lobby and live musicians soon would take the stage.

"Best of all," he said, "the honored guests of the festival, including Mr. Girard himself, will be mingling, too. So you'll be partying *with stars in your midst*!"

More frantic clapping. It's a wonder people weren't keeling over with excitement. I felt a little faint myself.

"Oh, Harley! We've got to find Mr. Girard in the crowd!"

"We will, hon. We will."

Chapter 8

It was chaos, of course. You can't offer four hundred people food, beverages and *celebrities* and expect them to behave themselves. The exits instantly became clogged with irritable people in uncomfortable shoes. Others clumped around the celebrities who'd been introduced in the audience. So many clamoring fans waved autograph books and cameras and business cards, you couldn't even see which celebrity they surrounded until you fought your way to the middle of the pile.

Fortunately, Harley is great in crowds. He's always very polite, but he has this *mass* and he knows how to use it. He leans into people, and they give way. In this manner, we plowed through several knots of goofballs, uncovering lesser lights at their cores, including that hairy director, Sean Hyde, who looked bored as people yammered at him about zombies.

As if the combined force of four hundred excited voices weren't enough noise, a mariachi band marched out onto the stage and launched into a brassy version of "La Bamba." It sounded like a cross between a traffic jam and a prison riot.

Harley said "excuse me" about a hundred times, always moving, me right on his heels, until we reached a curtained door beside the stage. An usher in a tuxedo cut us off at the pass. He was an impressively stoic young man who looked as if he spent his spare time lifting Volkswagens. Other fans had massed in front of him, trying to argue their way past, but the usher was unswerving.

"Think we ought to go around to the other end of the stage? Maybe they'll come out there."

"I don't know, Loretta." Harley looked over the milling throng. "This whole thing is a pig's breakfast, near as I can tell."

Disorder is the natural enemy of a man in the hardware business. If Harley had been in charge, there would've been a reception line and a food line and a beverage line, each separated by ropes, and people would've lined up alphabetically and/or by descending height. To really make him happy, we'd draw outlines on the floor so people would know exactly where to put their feet.

I'm okay with a little disorder, as my housework would attest, but Harley was right about this party. It was a mess. Sweaty people jostled and shoved and stepped on hems as they randomly tromped around the theater in search of sustenance and stardust. Neckties and hairdos came undone. Tempers flared.

Roger Sherwood (that rat) popped through the curtained door where we waited, a smarmy grin on his face. Frustrated festivalgoers immediately surrounded him four-deep. The knot of jabbering fans followed him toward the lobby, and Harley and I filled the gap, figuring more than ever that we were in the right place.

The beefy usher frowned at us, but Harley gave him his best Sunday-morning smile and leaned further into the usher's "bubble." I tell you, the man is a master.

Then the velvet curtain was cast aside, and we were face to face with Andre de Carlo and Tony Lodge, who were still dressed like the Devil and Humpty-Dumpty.

People around us immediately started throwing complaints at the festival organizers. Andre and Tony cowered in the doorway as the usher put out his arm to keep the rude throng from surging forward. Andre gibbered some assurance or the other, but I didn't hear the details. My attention was on the dozen people crowded into the wings beyond Andre and Tony. Because there, through a narrow gap between revelers, I caught a glimpse of silvery hair. I leaned to the left to see better and, sure enough, there was my idol.

Mr. Girard stood with his hands in his pockets, relaxed and confident as always, a wry smile on his face as he listened to Maria Mondragon, who was standing way too close to him, in my opinion. Granted, it was close quarters back there, but people should maintain some personal boundaries. Maria wore a slinky dress with black lace around the shoulders (why do young women think they're supposed to wear *lingerie* to formal events?), and she tossed her curly hair as she laughed at something he said.

The heavy curtain closed before I could see more. Andre and Tony elbowed their way toward the lobby, trailing gripers, and the muscular usher blocked the doorway again.

"I saw him!" I told Harley. "I saw Mr. Girard! He's right in there!"

"Okay, hon. Settle down. He'll be out in a minute."

"I don't know." I leaned closer and lowered my voice. "He looked *pretty* cozy back there, chatting with that girl from the film commission."

"She's young enough to be his granddaughter."

"Old enough to throw herself at him, apparently. Their noses were about three inches apart."

"Don't jump to conclusions, Loretta. Just because they were standing close doesn't mean they were flirting. I'm standing close to this usher, and we've got no personal chemistry going at all. Right, bud?"

The usher didn't even smile.

"She was laughing, too," I said bitterly. "Both of them were."

"Oh, well, that's different. Laughing together. That's a sure sign they're up to no good."

"Sarcasm is not your strong suit, Harley."

We stood in silence for a minute, both glaring at the usher, but that was as unsatisfying as taking it out on a robot, and pretty soon Harley sighed and draped his arm around my shoulders.

"Hang in there, hon. I'm sure Mr. Girard will be out any minute. We've just got to be patient."

"Easy for you to say," I grumped. "You're not wearing three-inch heels."

"True, but these loafers are pinching good. Does that count?"

I gave him a little squeeze around the middle.

"You're such a good sport," I said. "I know you must be starving. The food in the lobby will be long-gone before we get there."

"I can wait until we get back to the hotel. We can get room service."

He bobbed his eyebrows suggestively, which cracked me up. I nudged him with my hip and said, "If you play your cards right."

Then the curtain flung open again and the doorway was filled by The Other Man in My Life.

Michael Girard's easy smile was unshaken by the noise and flashbulbs that greeted him. Hilda Schmidt was right on his heels, looking like a broom wrapped in a blue gown, bless her heart. No sign of Maria Mondragon, which was just as well.

Others pressed forward, trying to reach Mr. Girard, but Harley hadn't been first-string varsity tackle at Pandora High School for nothing. He stepped sideways, blocking a woman dressed in beaded buckskin (no, I don't know why), and gave a hip-check to a young man who made the mistake of looking down at his iPhone, leaving his flank vulnerable.

Harley still had one hand on my shoulder, and he steered me into the hole he'd made. Right in front of Mr. Girard.

The noise fell away, drowned out by my own rapid heartbeat. My breath whistled in my nose, and I was sure Mr. Girard could hear it, despite the din behind me. I realized I was blinking rapidly, as if I were having some sort of medical emergency.

"Look, Mr. Girard," said Hilda, that dear, sweet girl. "It's Loretta Kimball!"

"Yes, it is," he said. "Hello, Loretta! Good to see you again."

I stopped blinking and melted right down into my shoes. He recognized me!

(Okay, all of Mr. Girard's assistants undoubtedly are trained to shout out people's names like that, but I saw the way Mr. Girard's eyes lit up, and there was no doubt in my mind that he really did remember me from our two previous encounters. You can imagine how special that made me feel. Of all the many faces that pass before Mr. Girard's eyes every single day, he remembered mine.)

I tried to say something about the fan club, but was handicapped by my smile, which had frozen in place. I must've looked like a ventriloquist's dummy. One with a stammer.

"I believe we're doing an interview in the morning," Mr. Girard said, turning the full force of his smile on me. "I'm looking forward to it."

I squeaked something about how I was, too. People still were shouting all around us, so who knows if he heard? I was in real danger of slipping into that tunnel-vision thing when this *presence* swooped in from my right, trampling our fledgling conversation.

Blinding sparkles. A gaucho hat.

Mitzi Tyner. And Nannette Hoch right beside her, cheery as the Ghost of Christmas Past.

"Mr. Gira-r-r-rd!" Mitzi brayed. "So lovely to see you! I'm your biggest fan!"

(Okay, stop right there. We all know that's not true. Mitzi Tyner wouldn't know Michael Girard from Ted Bundy if *I* were not in fact his biggest fan. My lifelong volunteer activity with the International Michael Girard Fan Club, ranging from the earliest mimeographed newsletters to my current nine terms as president, always has been kept separate from my life in Pandora. It was, therefore, the one part of my life untouched by Mitzi Tyner. And now she was trying to pee all over that, too, by barging in on my Big Moment.)

"Loretta?" she said girlishly. "Aren't you going to properly introduce me?"

"No," I said. "I am not."

She laughed gaily as she glittered ever closer to Mr. Girard.

"Loretta is such a *card*! We've known each other forever, and she's *always* been that way! We're both from the same town, a little place called Pandora, New Mexico. Have you heard of it?"

Mr. Girard opened his mouth to reply, but he wasn't quick enough. Mitzi had gotten a new lungful.

"My name is Mitzi Tyner, and my husband owns the Chevrolet dealership there in Pandora. If you're ever out our way, you should stop by and see him. He'd make you a real nice deal on a pickup truck."

A pickup truck. As if someone as urbane as Mr. Girard would be caught dead in a pickup truck. My God, I was mortified.

"This is my dear friend Nannette Hoch," Mitzi said. "She's from Pandora, too."

Nannette held out a limp hand for Mr. Girard to shake and I thought, *No, don't touch her, she'll suck the life right out of you*, but of course I couldn't say that out loud. He survived the handshake and glanced around, as if trying to find a way to extricate himself from these Pandora people. And who could blame him? Look at us: A braying bat in a flat-brimmed hat. A sad sack. A sweaty man in a rumpled tuxedo and foggy eyeglasses. And me, with my crazy hair and my damp green gown and my hinged mouth and my stupid, stupid friends.

Mr. Girard gave me a little smile, and said, "I must do my duty and mingle now. I'll see you tomorrow, Loretta."

He gracefully sidestepped us, plunging into the rabble, shaking hands and smiling and acting genuinely glad to be surrounded by yapping, wild-eyed film fanatics.

Hilda Schmidt followed so close behind him, she could've been mistaken for a papoose. She slipped me a wave before the crowd swallowed them up completely.

"'Tomorrow?'" Mitzi said. "What's happening tomorrow, Loretta?"

Harley grasped my arm.

Just in time, too.

Chapter 9

By the time Harley and I reached the lobby, the buffet had been reduced to an aftermath of crumbs and toothpicks and crumpled napkins. The waiters cleaning up the trashed tables had the dazed look of tornado victims.

Harley still held my elbow, steadily steering me toward the exit. Keeping me away from Mitzi Tyner. Keeping me away from Mr. Girard, too, if truth be told. I wanted to fight through the crowd for another shot at an audience with Mr. Girard, one in which I could make a better impression. But, as Harley pointed out more than once: "The man said he'd see you tomorrow."

So what if Mitzi ruined the gala? Tomorrow, I'd get an *entire hour* with Mr. Girard. Just the two of us (and, okay, maybe Hilda). No way could Mitzi horn in on that.

A refreshing wind slapped our faces as we stepped outside, and I pulled my green stole tighter around my shoulders. Other partiers spilled out onto the sidewalk around us, griping and gasping for air. Young men huffed and shot their cuffs. Near-naked girls squealed at the sudden chill. Limos crept along the curb like black sharks, swallowing up passengers. Harley steered me to a crosswalk, where we risked our lives to reach the other side of the street.

"You can let go of my arm now, Harley."

"You sure? This sidewalk's pretty uneven and it's dark and all."

"Let *me* hold *your* arm," I said. "That might help."

He hesitated.

"I'm not going to sprint back across the street in my high heels, Harley. I'm okay now."

"You're sure?"

"I will not allow Mitzi Tyner to get my goat."

"Good for you."

"She feeds on attention," I said as we resumed walking. "Making a scene would play right into her psychosis."

"That's a very mature attitude, Loretta."

"Thank you."

A dark figure rounded the corner up ahead, walking rapidly toward us. I felt Harley tense, then the stranger stepped into a shaft of spilled light and we could see it was the slick Hollywood producer, Kip Kaplin. He was dressed all in black, and his skinny eyeglasses reflected the streetlight glow. He wiped his nose with the back of his hand and said, "Hey, I know you two. You're friends with Hilda, right? Mr. Girard's assistant?"

"That's right," I said. "We met earlier. You're the one who wants to make the Western."

He grinned. "That's me. It's going to be a great movie. Working title is 'Thunder Canyon.'"

Harley and I exchanged a loaded look, then Harley said to him, "Weren't you at the gala?"

"I had some calls to make. Party still going on?"

"Winding down fast. Food's all gone."

"Michael Girard still there?"

"He was fifteen minutes ago."

"I'd better get back."

He hurried away without so much as a "thank you," and Harley and I waited until he was out of earshot before commenting on what a hyped-up weirdo he was. I guess it takes a high-energy person to be a Hollywood producer.

Other disheveled revelers were drifting toward the hotel, but we didn't recognize anyone else, which suited me fine. I'd had enough social interaction for one night.

We went into the overheated lobby, where Harley's glasses immediately steamed over. While he was cleaning them, that same skinny bellhop appeared out of nowhere and said, "Welcome to the Hotel Kokopelli."

"Thank you," I said. "We're already staying here."

"No bags," Harley said.

The bellhop skipped off to accost the next group coming through the door.

"That kid's gonna grow up to be a Wal-Mart greeter," Harley grumbled.

"I think he's going places. A positive outlook can accomplish a lot."

Harley scanned the lobby loiterers as we crossed to the elevators, alert for hazards.

"Really, Harley, I'm fine. You can relax."

He pressed the "up" button, and said, "I'll relax when I've got you behind closed doors. All to myself."

"I like the sound of that. Room service?"

"I was thinking we should go straight to dessert," he said.

"Is that so?" I looked around, but nobody was close enough to hear. "What did you have in mind?"

"I'll bet they have fresh strawberries at a swanky hotel like this."

The doors slid open, and we stepped into an empty elevator.

"Strawberries," I said. "That's what you want. Room-service strawberries."

"We could order the whipped cream without strawberries, but that might be too obvious."

"Oh, Harley." I nudged him with my elbow. "You devil."

"Heh-heh."

He gave my behind a little squeeze, which isn't like him at all. Even in the privacy of an elevator. They have cameras in those things.

"What's got you so worked up?"

"I don't know. Maybe it was seeing the way you look at Michael Girard."

That pulled me up short. I glanced over at him, instantly worried, but found him smiling.

"Oh, Harley, you know better than--"

"A lesser man might let that bother him, but not me."

I squeezed his arm.

"If you were a lesser man, you wouldn't be married to me."

FAN FAIR: THE OFFICIAL WEBSITE OF THE INTERNATIONAL MICHAEL GIRARD FAN CLUB

7:24 a.m. March 25

From the President:

Good morning! The second day of the Santa Fe Silver Screen Society Film Festival starts momentarily, so just a quick note to summarize the activities so far.

The opening gala was a little disappointing, I must say. The organizers (if you could call them that) underestimated the size and appetite of the audience. Four hundred people filled the Zia Theater, and they generally behaved like a horde of locusts. And the gala was plagued by the sort of technical difficulties that you'd expect at a first-time event.

Despite all that, it was delightful to see, up close and personal, such celebrities as Ava Andrews and our own Michael Girard. They looked lovely on stage together, and were so gracious when they were mobbed afterward.

My husband and I exchanged hellos with Mr. Girard and his personal assistant, Hilda Schmidt, but we had to keep it brief because so many ravenous fans wanted some of his time. This morning, I get my *hour*-long interview with Mr. Girard, and I will be asking questions suggested by you fans over the past few weeks.

Today's film festival events include screenings of two movies starring Mr. Girard ("Hell's Britches" and the historical classic "The Meek"), as well as an appearance by Ms. Andrews, his former co-star on "Empire."

I will, of course, give you updates as time and events merit.

Sincerely,
Loretta Kimball, president, IMGFC

Chapter 10

It was a thrill, I confess, to push the elevator button marked "P." The penthouse was only one floor above the one where Harley and I were staying, and the elevators went up there without any special cardkey or anything. But how often does the average person venture into a "penthouse?"

I trembled during the brief elevator ride, anticipating my session with Mr. Girard, crushing my notebook to my bosom like a schoolgirl. My mini-recorder and camera were in my shoulder bag, which weighed about ten pounds. I'd dressed in business casual -- nice jeans, flats, a red blazer over a black cashmere sweater -- and my curly hair was behaving itself. I'd drunk three cups of coffee already, and all my questions and preparations pinged around inside my skull like Lotto balls. Also, I wished I'd peed before I left our room.

All such thoughts vanished when the elevator doors slid open onto a corridor crowded with police and paramedics and bewildered guests in bathrobes.

"Oh, my God!" I said to the nearest policeman. "What's happened?"

He was a tall man whose black uniform bore lots of gold touches to indicate rank, and his nametag was filled with one of those unpronounceable Polish names that make you want to buy a vowel. He looked down his long nose at me, and his eyes settled on the notebook in my hand.

"You a reporter?"

"What? No! I'm a guest in this hotel. Why is this hallway blocked?"

(I believe in taking the offensive when it comes to authority figures. Ask Llano County Sheriff Luke Johnson, who has given me more warning tickets than anyone in the history of Pandora.)

"There's been a problem on this floor," the cop said. "You'll have to find another way to your room."

"But I've got an appointment with Mr. Girard."

His eyes narrowed. "Girard? Now?"

I didn't appreciate the sneer on his face, but before I could tell him so, we were interrupted by someone calling my name.

I turned to find Hilda Schmidt headed our way. She wore a short white robe with a Hotel Kokopelli crest. Her legs and feet were bare. Her brown hair needed brushing, and her eyes were bloodshot.

"It's okay, Officer," she said. "Loretta's with me."

He clearly didn't think much of that. "Is she staying on this floor?"

"Loretta's the president of Mr. Girard's fan club," Hilda said. "She was supposed to interview him this morning."

He frowned. "We're trying to contain the fallout here. As you people requested."

Don't you hate that? "You people." How rude. To her credit, Hilda didn't sink to his level.

"I'll need all the help I can get when the media gets wind of this," she said. "At least we know Loretta's on our side."

I had no idea what she was talking about, or why we might be choosing up teams, but I nodded vigorously. I *was* on Mr. Girard's side, no matter what.

"All right," the officer said after a moment. "But she's your responsibility."

Hilda grabbed my sleeve and dragged me past the room where the police and plainclothesmen were going in and out. A half-dozen hotel guests buzzed nearby. The only one I recognized was Kip Kaplin, the movie producer, who looked bleary, as if mornings were unfamiliar to him.

The corridor was lined with a half-dozen doors per side, and we walked nearly to the other end before Hilda leaned close enough to whisper in my ear.

"That crime scene is Mr. Girard's room."

"No!" My heart fluttered. "Is he okay?"

"Yes, yes. But the police are questioning him."

"About *what*?"

"A dead woman," she whispered. "In his suite."

"Oh, sweet Jesus."

Hilda shivered inside the terry-cloth robe. I wrapped my arms around her bony shoulders and held her close, exactly the way I used to hold Jessica when she came home from a bad day

88

at school. Sometimes, a hug is the only thing that'll help.

I softly patted her back, cooing that everything would be all right and we'd get it sorted out and other reassuring nonsense. Meanwhile, my mind whirled. A *dead* woman? In Mr. Girard's room?

"Was it natural causes?" I offered gently. "A heart attack, something like that?"

"Her forehead has a big dent in it."

"Oh, my God."

Hilda leaned back to look me in the eye. Her face was streaked with tears.

"Oh, Loretta, what are we going to do? The tabloids will be all over us. They'll try to *ruin* Mr. Girard."

"Take it easy, darling. We'll get through it, whatever's happened."

She looked ready to tune up again, so I tried to divert her. "Why are you still in your robe?"

"I didn't take time to dress," she said. "Mr. Girard called the police, then he called me next. When I got to his suite, the body was still on the sofa. He'd covered her with a sheet, but I could see her bare feet. They were so pale."

She choked up, and I applied hugs until she was able to continue.

"Mr. Girard said he had no idea how she got there, he'd been asleep in the other room. Then the police showed up and separated us. They've kept him behind closed doors ever since."

I checked the corridor. That producer, Kip Kaplin, had edged closer, but he wasn't near enough to eavesdrop. Some of the cops were looking our way, too, curious about all the whispering.

While I had the chance, I asked Hilda, "Do you know who the dead woman was?"

She nodded, gulping. "You know her, too."

I gasped.

"It's that girl from the film commission. Maria Mondragon."

Chapter 11

Poor Maria. So young and vibrant yesterday, so sure of herself. And now she's *dead*? Even as I tried to console Hilda, my thoughts were a runaway train. Was it an accident? A *murder*? Why would anyone want to kill Maria? And how in holy hell did she end up in Mr. Girard's suite?

She'd been flirting with Mr. Girard backstage. Had something sparked between them? Had she come to his room in the night? Some women lose their minds around celebrities, and Mr. Girard has so much natural charisma--

"Hey, ladies." Kip Kaplin had sneaked up on us. "Everything okay here?"

Just the sort of stupid question a man would ask. I held Hilda closer and said, "Give us a minute, please."

I had more questions for Hilda, now that her weeping had settled to the occasional hiccup, but out here in the hallway, with Kip hovering, was not the place to ask them.

"Hilda?" I said. "You'd feel better if you put on some clothes. Where's your room?"

She pointed to a room two doors down from Mr. Girard's. I kept a protective arm around her as we walked there. She produced a cardkey from the pocket of her robe, and we went inside.

It was a regular hotel room, a little bigger than ours, but nothing too elaborate. But it did have a beautiful view across rooftops to the sun-gilt towers of St. Francis Cathedral.

I got busy with the room's miniature coffeemaker while Hilda sniffled through the clothes hanging neatly in her closet. She carried some jeans and a dark blue blouse into the bathroom, and left the door ajar so we could talk while she dressed.

"I saw Maria with Mr. Girard at the theater last night," I said. "But I assumed he left there with you."

"He *did*. He was exhausted after all that glad-handing. It really wears him out. We came back upstairs, and he went into his suite. *Alone*."

"Maybe Maria visited him after one of the late-night parties."

"Plenty of those on this floor last night," Hilda said. "Lots of noise."

"Maybe Mr. Girard couldn't sleep."

She snorted. "He can *always* sleep. Ten hours straight, every night. It's the secret to his youthful looks."

"Must be nice. I can't remember the last time I slept more than--"

"His doctor gives him these little white pills. Two at bedtime, and he can sleep through earthquakes."

The bathroom door opened wider. Hilda was dressed, if still barefoot, and running a brush through her hair. I could see her face reflected in the mirror above the black granite sink.

"Mr. Girard told me he doesn't remember anything happening during the night," she said. "He locked the door, went to bed and had a good night's sleep. Got up this morning and found Maria dead on his sofa. No idea how she got there."

That, I knew, would not fly with the police. Or the press. Women don't magically appear in hotel suites, dead or alive. Somebody let her in that door.

"Maybe she bribed a bellhop or a maid," I said. "Got 'em to let her into the suite so she could surprise Mr. Girard."

"Maybe. But that wouldn't explain how--"

Someone pounded on the door, making us both jump.

"Police! Open up!"

Hilda froze in place, so I opened the door. I was nearly bowled over by two men in off-the-rack brown suits. They had badges hanging on chains around their necks.

"What are you two doing in here?" shouted the older one, a jowly bald man with a mustache so dark it looked painted on.

I said, "I beg your pardon--"

"Who are you?" His breath smelled like burnt coffee. "What are you doing in here?"

"She's getting dressed," I snapped. "Or she was, until you so rudely burst into this room."

He squinted at me. His eyebrows were extra-dark, too, as if making up for his shiny scalp.

His partner was twenty years younger, Hispanic, short black hair, no distinguishing marks. Almost handsome, but all his features were slightly *off*: His ears stuck out a tad too much and his fleshy nose seemed to fit a different face. His close-set eyes had a slightly unfocused look, as if he were struggling to keep up.

"What's wrong with him?" I asked.

Baldy clamped his mouth shut, and his scalp turned red. I half-expected steam to come out of his ears, like in a cartoon.

"Nothing's wrong with him. He's *new*."

The young man blushed and thrust out his hand.

"Detective Rick Torres," he said, and there was real pride in the way he said "detective."

His partner rolled his eyes.

"This is Senior Detective Nelson Boyd," Torres said. "I'm not as new as he lets on. I've been with the department for ten years."

"Yeah, and you've been a detective for ten minutes. Question these women. I want to know what they were doing in this room."

Torres fumbled with a little notebook, then asked Hilda, "What were you doing in this room?"

"Getting dressed."

That seemed good enough for Torres, but Boyd blustered at her, "I told you to wait in the hall."

"It's freezing out there! I needed shoes."

"You're still barefoot," Torres offered. A real Sherlock, this kid.

"Excuse me," I said. "Detective Boyd? If I may? I was in here the entire time and I can testify that Miss Schmidt did nothing wrong. She simply put on some decent clothes. I don't believe that's too much to ask, considering that this young woman has been through such a traumatic event."

Boyd's eyes got wider the longer I talked. By the time I ran out of breath, they looked as if they might pop from their sockets.

"Who *are* you?"

"My name is Loretta Kimball, and I am a citizen of Pandora, New Mexico, and I know my rights."

"Aw, hell," Boyd said. "One of those."

"You cannot simply order a person to stand around in a chilly hotel corridor half-naked for hours," I said. "That is both cruel and unusual. Also, it is no way to treat a witness."

"What about a *suspect*?" Boyd wheeled on Hilda, as if that would trick her into a weeping confession. Instead, she about jumped out of her skin.

"Stop yelling at people," I said. "That's no way to behave."

Boyd swallowed whatever smartass thing he'd started to say, and instead, speaking with a creepy calm, said, "I want to know what she's doing here."

Okay, now that stymied me. I wasn't sure which "she" he was talking about, or whether he was still speaking to me or to Hilda, but before I could sort it out, Torres said, "What are you doing here, Mrs. Kimball?"

"I was scheduled to meet with Mr. Girard this morning." I checked my wristwatch. "Ten minutes ago. But when I got off the elevator, I found that his suite was full of police. I saw Hilda and she was upset and I suggested that she'd feel better if she were dressed, so we came in here and she jumped into some jeans, but honestly we'd only been in this room two minutes when you knocked on the door."

Torres raised a hand to stop me.

"You're not staying on this floor?"

"No, we're one floor down. My husband Harley and me. Oh, I should call Harley. If he hears about this before--"

"Take your hand out of your purse, ma'am."

"What?"

Both detectives had pushed back their jackets and their hands were on the butts of pistols holstered to their hips. Big black pistols.

"Good heavens," I said. "What is *wrong* with you? I'm getting out my phone to call Harley."

Torres smiled, but he said, "Perhaps you could put your bag on the bed for now."

"Fine." I zipped my purse shut before I set it down. "There. Happy?"

Boyd looked from Hilda to me and back again. "I'm guessing Miss Schmidt told you what's happened here. I'd like to hear what she said."

We all looked to Torres. Flushing, he said, "What about that, Mrs. Kimball? What did she tell you?"

"Only that someone had died, and that was why so many police were here."

"Did she say who?" Boyd asked.

A pause.

I said to Torres, "Your serve."

He flushed deeper. "Well? Did she?"

"Oh, of course I did!" Hilda blurted. "What kind of stupid question is that? Loretta, who is my *friend*, finds me crying at a *crime scene*, it's only natural that she'd ask me who died."

"Were you surprised to hear that Miss Mondragon was dead?"

Boyd slapped a palm to his forehead, then ran his hand down his rubbery face.

"Yes, I was surprised," I said.

"Why is that?"

"Because she was what, twenty-two years old? Not exactly at death's door. How did she die anyway?"

Torres muttered something about awaiting an autopsy, and Boyd shot him a withering look.

"Was she even staying in this hotel?" I asked.

Hilda shook her head, but Boyd barked, "We ask the questions. Not you."

Torres flipped pages in his notebook, trying to pick up the thread.

"Okay," he said after several tense seconds. "When was the last time you saw Mr. Girard?"

I assumed he was speaking to me, though he didn't look up from his scrawled notes. Surely, they'd already asked Hilda about the last time *she* saw Mr. Girard.

"Last night at the gala," I said. "Just as he started mingling with the audience."

"You didn't see him back here at the hotel?"

"No."

"What about Miss Mondragon?"

"Same story." I said this matter-of-factly, but my heart did a little skitter. "Saw her at the gala, but not back here at the hotel."

Torres appeared to ponder this, buying time, but Boyd couldn't stand it any longer.

"Go back to the reason we were looking for Miss Schmidt."

It took Torres a second to remember, but then he asked Hilda, "You have a key to Mr. Girard's suite?"

She stiffened. "I *told* you that already. He always gives me his spare key, in case of emergency."

Boyd demanded that she produce the room key, and Hilda opened the satchel-like purse I'd seen her carrying the day before.

"I notice no one pulls a gun on *her* when she goes for her handbag," I said archly, but the cops ignored me.

"Just dump it on the bed, please," Torres said.

Hilda upended the bag, exposing the usual embarrassing detritus of lipsticks and tampons and tattered Kleenex. No guns or knives, so the detectives let her poke through the stuff until she unearthed the cardkey.

"Don't touch it," Torres said quickly. He pulled a plastic bag out of his pocket and deftly scooped the cardkey inside.

"Maybe someone took this from her purse," he said to Boyd. "And that's how they got into Girard's suite."

"And then they put it *back* in her purse?"

"Maybe," Torres said. "To cover their tracks."

He turned to Hilda and said, "Was this handbag out of your sight at all last night?"

"No."

"You're sure?"

"Yes."

"Hmm."

Boyd said something about checking the cardkey for fingerprints, but it didn't sound promising. Torres looked stumped.

These were the detectives in charge of clearing Mr. Girard? These two goofballs? I looked at Hilda and our eyes met, and I could tell she was thinking the same thing.

Mr. Girard was in big trouble.

Chapter 12

After Hilda stepped into some shoes, the detectives herded us back into the hall and ordered us to stay put. I started to object, but Boyd snarled something unintelligible and I decided to keep quiet. For the moment.

The detectives disappeared into Mr. Girard's suite, and I gave Hilda another hug, mostly so I could get close enough to whisper, "Was that the truth, what you told them? Nobody could've taken that cardkey?"

She nodded.

"I'll bet somebody with the film festival gave a key to Maria."

"They reserved this whole floor for VIPs," she said.

I looked around the corridor. I still didn't recognize anyone other than Kip Kaplin (who was headed our way again), but the other civilians had a certain glow. Golden tans. Perfect haircuts. Funky shoes. Unquestionably film people.

Most had changed out of their hotel bathrobes while waiting to be turned loose. I wondered whether Boyd and Torres burst in on *them*, too. None of the guests seemed as shaken as I felt. Most were busy whispering into cell phones, no doubt spreading gossip around the country.

Which reminded me that I was going to call Harley.

"Are you okay, Hilda? Can you spare me a minute?"

She nodded, and I turned away, holding my cell at arm's length to see the buttons.

(Yes, I should get reading glasses, but I'm too vain. So far.)

"Hullo?"

Harley sounded like his mouth was full. Probably those waffles he'd been eyeballing earlier on the room-service menu.

"Harley, it's me. You'll never believe what's happened!"

"Hrm?"

I wandered down the hall, away from the others, so I wouldn't have to be so careful about whispering.

"Remember that girl Maria Mondragon? From the film commission?"

"Mm-hm."

"She's *dead*!"

Harley made a sound that I took to be a gulp of surprise, though it might've been swallowing.

"Holy shit! What happened to her?"

"Conked on the head. And Mr. Girard was the one who found the body!"

"Holy shit. Where did he find it?"

"In his suite."

"He *found* her there? He didn't know she was in his own room?"

"It's a two-room suite. She was on the sofa. The police are still sorting it out. I was just interviewed by detectives."

"You *what*?"

"Interviewed. I was with Hilda, bless her heart, and these idiot detectives demanded to know who I was and all that."

I looked over my shoulder to make sure those idiots hadn't come up behind me. The coast was clear, but I noticed Hilda was pinned against the wall by an emphatically whispering Kip Kaplin. What could that pushy man want now?

Harley was saying something about how I ought to stay out of police business, but I cut him off.

"Mr. Girard needs me. So does Hilda. She said as much."

"Needs you to do what?"

"Hold her hand through this crisis. Maybe help her with the newspaper and TV people."

"Oh, hell," he said. "I hadn't even thought about reporters. They'll be all over this."

"Those buzzards."

"I'm sure that's not the attitude Hilda wants you to project."

"Oh, I know. But I can fake it. I'll put on a big smile, and I'll talk and talk, and I'll tell those reporters exactly nothing."

"You can do that?"

I could tell he was kidding me.

"It'll be just like a church social," I said. "For now, though, I'm stuck here on the penthouse floor."

"They're *holding* you there?"

"They told us to wait in the hall. There's a bunch of us here."

I glanced over at Hilda and Kip. I couldn't hear what he was saying, but she was shaking her head.

"I'd better go. I think Hilda needs me."

"Wait," he said. "Should I come up there?"

"No, finish your breakfast. Things will clear up here soon."

I headed toward Hilda.

"Okay," Harley said. "Too bad about that Maria, though. She seemed like a nice kid."

"Yes, she did. I hope we can find out what happened to her."

"What do you mean 'we,' Loretta? Didn't you hear what I was saying about police business?"

"Of course, Harley. Don't worry about me. I'm no meddler."

He snorted, but I didn't give him a chance to dig himself into a hole.

"Got to go. I'll call you soon."

Kip took a step away from Hilda as I arrived. He seemed annoyed at the interruption.

"How you doing, sweetie?" I asked her. "Holding up all right?"

"I'm fine. Thanks."

She didn't seem fine. She looked flushed and sweaty, as if maybe running a low-grade fever. Probably just stress.

Clearly, Kip wanted me to move along, but I was having none of that. I threaded my arm through Hilda's and dragged her away from the wall.

"I need to speak to you privately," I said.

"Sure."

I looked back over my shoulder at Kaplin, but he was already dialing his phone to pester somebody else.

"Is that man bothering you?"

Hilda sighed. "He doesn't know how to take 'no' for an answer."

"He's trying to talk business? Even at a terrible time like this?"

"Some people have a problem with boundaries."

"Some people have a problem with manners." I glared at Kip Kaplin, but he'd turned away, so it was wasted. "I was giving you an escape if you needed one."

"Thanks, Loretta. I appreciate the thought. I may need a lot of rescuing over the next few days."

"You can count on me."

Chapter 13

Hilda had calls of her own to make, so I walked her to the end of the carpeted corridor, where she could get some privacy. After making sure Kip Kaplin was as far away as possible, I felt free to leave her alone.

I eased through the gawkers, trying to get a glimpse inside Mr. Girard's suite without being too obvious. I regretted the bright red blazer I'd chosen to wear, but who knew I'd need to be stealthy today?

The suite was abuzz with activity. Crime scene technicians in white coveralls and paper booties dusted for fingerprints and snapped flash photos, and it all would've been very exciting had I not been so worried for Mr. Girard.

The hallway VIPs whispered and speculated -- *What did Girard do to that girl? Why are the police still holding him?* -- and it was as if I could hear the murmuring spread coast to coast.

All those years in Hollywood, and Mr. Girard never generated the tiniest sliver of gossip. He finally comes to New Mexico, to *my* state, and look what happens.

I know that's a selfish attitude. I should've been thinking about Maria Mondragon and her family. But I'd waited weeks (okay, all my life) for my conversation with Mr. Girard, and naturally I was disappointed.

The uniformed officer just outside Mr. Girard's door carefully stared above our heads so we wouldn't be tempted to ask questions. No getting past him. The senior officer, the one with the impossible-to-pronounce name, was over by the elevators, not far from Kip Kaplin, who seemed uncomfortable to have a cop looming nearby.

An elevator went "ding!" As the doors slid open, the officer thrust out both arms, as if he could ward off whatever was about to spill out.

Well. He hadn't counted on the deluge that was Andre de Carlo, who flooded through the doors in a wave of tears and wailing.

"Oh, my God! This is *terrible*! The worst thing that could've possibly happened to me!"

Tony Lodge trailed behind Andre, looking like an egg in a cowboy hat. Both men had gone for the full Retro Rodeo look. Wide-brimmed hats, silver-tipped boots, *concha* belts and yoked satin shirts no self-respecting cowboy in his right mind would be caught dead in. Ever.

To top it off, Andre wore a suede jacket with long fringe on the chest and sleeves. The fringe whipped about as he fluttered and flailed. It's a wonder he didn't put somebody's eye out.

"Poor *Maria*!" he cried. "How I loved that girl! And now she's gone. Snuffed out like a candle in the wind!"

Tony patted his fringed shoulder, but Andre was in no mood to be consoled. Not when there was so much drama and cliché to be had. He carried on about how Maria would be missed, and how the film festival must struggle on without her.

"Sir," the senior officer finally interjected. "We need to keep this floor sealed off. This is an active crime scene--"

"Excuse me, but do you know who I am? I run this film festival. It's my baby. And now my baby has been *slain*! Right along with poor, poor Maria!"

Andre's histrionics attracted the attention of the officer next to Mr. Girard's door. He drifted toward the commotion, ready to back up his superior officer as he tried to corral the ever-louder *caballero*.

I saw my chance to sneak a peek inside the suite, and stepped right up to the doorway. The white-suited technicians paid no attention to me. They were too busy brushing and bagging and plucking up fibers with tweezers. One ran a hand vacuum over the burnished surface of a brown leather sofa.

My stars, I thought, that must be the sofa where Maria was found dead. Maybe even the spot where she actually *died*. I looked away rather than dwell on that.

The suite was decorated simply, with tile floors and plaster walls and rustic *vigas* overhead. Huge windows offered views of blue skies and snow-sugared mountains. The heavy furniture was dusty with gray fingerprint powder.

The door to the bedroom stood open, and it took only one more tiny step forward to see in there. My heart nearly stopped when I found Mr. Girard perfectly framed in the doorway.

He was sitting on the end of the rumpled bed, his head in his hands, the absolute picture of sadness and fatigue. He wore dress slacks and a blue shirt with black suspenders, but no tie, and battered corduroy slippers like your grandpa wore.

He must've sensed me watching. His head tipped up and he looked me right in the eye. It was as if he'd aged ten years overnight. His face sagged. His blue eyes were bloodshot.

But he recognized me, a familiar face in all this turmoil. A friend. His sad face creased into that famous charismatic smile, and I very nearly dropped dead on the spot.

Only lasted a moment. The doorway filled with Detective Nelson Boyd, his fat face twisted up like a bawling baby's as he shrieked at me.

"What the *hell* are you doing?"

"Uh." I glanced back at the corridor, which seemed very far away. Guess I'd drifted farther into the suite than I'd realized.

"What is going on here?" Boyd screamed. "Did none of you idiots see this woman walk right into your crime scene?"

The techs muttered and shrugged and averted their eyes.

"And you!" He wheeled to shout into my face. "Is there something *wrong* with you? Do you have a mental *defect* of some sort?"

I drew myself up to my full height (which was about the same as his) and said, "I most certainly do not."

"Then how is it you don't know that you're not supposed to saunter into a crime scene? Haven't you seen cop shows on TV? Do they *have* TV where you live?"

"I won't dignify that with--"

"I ought to place you under arrest right now."

"Oh, I am so sure. On what charge?"

"Criminal trespass." He started counting off on his fingers. I hate when people do that. "Interfering with a criminal investigation. Disobeying an officer. Destroying evidence."

He'd run out of fingers, so I said, "Might as well add 'resisting arrest.' I won't go quietly."

I tried to see if Mr. Girard was hearing this, but Detective Torres had filled up the bedroom doorway and I couldn't see past him. Torres was cringing, as if expecting a loud noise. But when Boyd answered me, his voice was weary and low.

"Lady, I imagine you've never done anything quietly in your life. Do you ever stop talking? I'll bet you talk in your sleep."

"I do not--"

"I feel sorry for your husband."

"You can leave my husband out of this," I snapped. "We have been happily married for twenty-four years, thank you very much."

Boyd's smirk smeared his mustache all over his face.

"If you're so happily married," he said. "What are you doing in here, making eyes at Michael Girard?"

"Oh, I was not!" My face felt hot, and I knew I must be bright red. "I came to see if I could help in any way. If Mr. Girard needs anything. You people have kept him penned up in here all morning--"

Boyd held up his hand to stop me.

"I don't want to hear it. I want you out of my crime scene. I want you off this floor."

I tried for a last look at Mr. Girard, but I still couldn't see past Torres.

"Go," Boyd commanded. "Now."

"I'm going, I'm going."

I backed away, Boyd matching me step for step. His jowls bounced in chewing motions, though his mouth seemed empty of gum. Maybe he was chewing his own tongue.

Noise was rising in the hall. Boyd shouted, "What the *hell*?" He pushed past me into the corridor.

Andre and Tony stood back-to-back near the elevators, surrounded by three uniformed officers. Andre had lost his cowboy hat, and his hair whipped around, wild as the fringe on his jacket. He appeared to be fending off the cops with a potted rubber plant.

"Stay back!" he screamed, swinging the three-foot-tall plant and strewing bits of potting soil all over the carpet. "I am *distraught*, and you cannot manhandle me!"

No one seemed to be manhandling him, though the officers clearly were frustrated with the hysteria.

"*Hey!*" Boyd stormed into the middle of the melee, and snatched the plant out of Andre's hands. "What the fuck is the matter with you?"

The detective pitched the plant aside, and it crashed into a corner.

"Aw," I said, "there's no reason to do that. That plant hadn't done anything."

(I know, I know. I should learn to keep my mouth shut. But after years in the Garden Society, I can't stand by and watch someone abuse an innocent houseplant.)

Boyd ignored me, too busy barking at Tony and Andre. "You two cowboys get back on that elevator and ride it downstairs before I put on my spurs and kick your asses all over this hotel."

Tony the Egg worked up enough yolk to say, "That would be police brutality."

"So? That's my favorite kind of brutality."

Andre and Tony shrank back. One of the officers must've pushed the button because the elevator doors slid open and the festival organizers backed right inside.

Boyd grabbed my elbow and dragged me over to the elevator, too.

"Here, take her with you. All you loudmouths can entertain each other."

I started to object, but realized that would only prove his point. Instead, I glared at him until the doors closed completely.

Tony shuddered. "What a horrible man."

"You said it, Tex."

Chapter 14

In all the excitement, I'd forgotten to pee. My bladder sent urgent reminders as I hustled off the elevator and down the long corridor to our room. I dug in my purse for my cardkey, but saw that was hopeless and banged on the door instead.

Harley was dressed for the day, but his hair was still wet. The air that whooshed out of the room smelled of Aqua Velva and maple syrup.

"Loretta! Are you okay?"

"No! Move out of the way!"

He looked puzzled, but did as he was told, and I shot past him. The sticky remains of his room-service breakfast covered a cart parked in front of the TV, which silently displayed a news show. Still a little steamy in the bathroom, but that didn't interfere with my needs. I was much more relaxed when I emerged two minutes later.

Harley stood by the TV, twisting the remote control in his hands, looking worried.

"Are you okay, hon? Are you sick?"

"Just sick at heart, Harley."

He gathered me up in a comforting hug.

"That poor girl," I said. "Taken so young."

"I know, hon. It's a terrible thing."

He kissed my forehead and said, "So the police turned you loose?"

"A rude detective ordered me to leave."

"He ordered you to leave."

"Yes. I've half a mind to write to the chief of police regarding his behavior."

Harley squinted at me. "What did you do, Loretta?"

"Whatever could you mean?"

"One minute, the police won't let you leave. The next, they won't let you stay. Sounds like Hurricane Loretta to me."

"I've told you before, Harley. I do not care for that little nickname."

"Sorry, hon."

"I sort of walked into the crime scene," I admitted. "Completely unintentional, but you know how I am. Just looking around, and my feet went in there on their own. Detective Boyd wouldn't listen to any such explanation, of course. He was too busy blowing his top."

"I can imagine."

"You should see this man, Harley. A little pressure cooker. Steam hissing off him all the time."

"I hope you didn't say *that* to him."

"Who gets a chance to say anything around that man? I could barely get a word in."

Harley's lips disappeared into his mouth, and I recognized that he was making an effort to withhold comment.

"Forget Boyd," I said. "He and his partner are idiots. They'll never figure out who killed Maria Mondragon."

Harley's eyes widened. "So it's murder, for sure?"

"Hilda said Maria had a big dent in her forehead."

"Maybe she fell. Hit something on the way down."

"I doubt that very much. I think it's more likely somebody clubbed her with something."

Harley started to argue, but I hate when he gets all logical and explanatory. (Don't ever, ever ask him a hardware question unless you've got ten minutes to listen to the complete answer.)

"*Either way*," I said, "her body was found in Mr. Girard's room, and that's the real mystery here. Mr. Girard doesn't know how she got there. Hilda had the other key to his suite, and she didn't let Maria in there. But somebody unlocked that door for her. And then they killed her there!"

He squinched up his face. Harley hates gory stuff. I always have to watch bloody movies by myself.

"It was just a whack on the head, Harley. They didn't cut her up with a chainsaw."

Squinch.

"I didn't see anything in the room that could've been used as a weapon, but maybe the police had already bagged up the evidence."

"Loretta--"

"It doesn't take much to kill somebody. Any blunt instrument will do, if you swing it hard enough."

That gave Harley pause. His hardware-trained mind busily inventoried the hotel room, finding the right tool for the job.

"Steam iron," he said. "You could brain somebody with that."

"What about a champagne bottle?" I offered. "Plenty of those floating around last night."

"Sure, that would do it. But wouldn't Mr. Girard have heard something? I mean, if Maria was being clubbed in the next room, that should've woke him up."

"Hilda says he takes sleeping pills every night. He never wakes up."

"Somebody must've heard something. I can't imagine Maria went down without a fight."

"She was a spirited young woman. But maybe she wasn't killed there. Maybe she died elsewhere, and her body was dumped in Mr. Girard's room."

"Why would somebody *do* that?"

"It would have to be somebody who really hated Mr. Girard. Somebody who had it in for him."

Roger Sherwood (that rat) flashed through my mind, but I couldn't picture him depositing a dead woman in Mr. Girard's suite. Might muss his hair.

"Wait a minute," Harley said. "You think somebody set this up just to make Mr. Girard look bad?"

"Well, it's possible--"

"Somebody would commit *murder* to generate bad publicity for an *actor*?"

"When you say it like that, it sounds silly."

"How would you say it?"

He was making me cross, so I opted to change the subject.

"Is there any more coffee? I made some in Hilda's room, but we never got a sip before those detectives rousted us."

"There's probably one cup left."

He lifted a carafe off the breakfast cart, feeling its weight, then nodded and poured me a cup.

I sat on the foot of the bed, overwhelmed and exhausted. Could barely work up the strength to hold the cup after Harley put cream and sugar in it for me.

"I feel so bad for Mr. Girard," I said. "This could *ruin* him. You know the tabloids will go crazy."

"Two people in a hotel suite. One of them ends up dead. It's only natural that he would be a suspect."

"But anyone who knows Mr. Girard knows he could never hurt another human being. Oh, you should've seen him, Harley! He looked so broken down, so *defeated*."

"When was this?"

"A few minutes ago. Upstairs. He was sitting on the bed, just as I am now, and he had his head in his hands. Just miserable. I wanted to comfort him, but that was when Detective Boyd spotted me and started yelling and it was time to go."

"Ah."

"What a horrid man. That's what Tony Lodge said about him in the elevator. 'Horrid.' The perfect word for him."

"Tony was with you?"

"Well, he was with Andre. But the three us were ejected from the penthouse floor together."

"What did they do to get kicked out?"

"Andre had a gibbering fit about how Maria died just to screw up his film festival. Very dramatic. Tony tried to calm him down."

"The usual."

"Yes, except Andre threatened the police with a potted plant."

Harley pointed at his ear. "Say that again. It sounded like you said 'potted plant.'"

"That's exactly what I said. A rubber tree, to be exact. Haven't you noticed the little rubber tree plants next to every elevator?"

Harley blinked twice.

"Andre's lucky the police didn't shoot him," I said. "If somebody came at me with a rubber plant, I'd be tempted to shoot him in the leg. But that would just make Andre cry louder, and nobody wanted to hear that."

Harley's attention drifted toward the television as I spoke, and he suddenly said, "Whoa." The screen displayed a publicity still of Michael Girard.

Harley pointed the remote at the TV and an anchorman's voice said, "Police in Santa Fe are investigating allegations involving veteran film and television actor Michael Girard. Initial reports are that a young woman has been found dead in Girard's hotel room. No details yet, but we have reporters en route."

As the screen switched to a different story, Harley hit the "mute" again.

"It's a *suite*," I said. "A two-room suite. With a door in between that was most likely closed all night. I *knew* they'd get it wrong. They'll make Mr. Girard look terrible."

"It's early yet," he said. "They're working off sketchy information. Maybe the police will get them straightened out."

I snorted indelicately. "You haven't seen these detectives. They couldn't find a suspect in broad daylight if he locked himself in their police car."

"Come on, Loretta. I'm sure they know what they're doing."

"Meanwhile, every reporter in the world is rushing to Santa Fe. I should let Hilda know the rumors are already leaking on cable news."

I slugged down the last of my coffee and started digging in my purse for my phone.

"Um. Maybe you should stay out of it, Loretta."

"Whatever do you mean?"

"You're already crossways with the police."

I stopped hunting for my phone and looked up at him.

"Hilda asked for my help. I can't just abandon her to the wolves."

"I know, hon, but--"

"I'm sure I can conduct myself in such a manner that I won't get thrown in jail."

"That's not what I meant and you know it."

"Are you worried I'll embarrass you, Harley?"

"Aw, that's not it at all. I just know how you are. You start off helping Hilda make a few phone calls, and before we know what hit us, you're conducting a full-scale investigation."

"I have no intention of--"

"You get carried away, Loretta. You know it's true."

We've had this talk many times before. I admit I am prone to passing enthusiasms. I'll get caught up in, say, knitting, and buy a bunch of supplies and make plans to knit my own Christmas gifts. But then I'll get interested in basket-weaving or bird-watching or something, and wander off. End up with a big pile of red and green yarn for which I have no use. I've got many such unfinished projects stacked around the house.

Harley insists that my focus has gotten more scattered since our children went off to college. He thinks I'm filling our empty nest with busywork and volunteerism so I won't feel lonely. I think he's exaggerating. Also, I suspect he's tired of me spending our disposable income on craft supplies.

"Don't start with me, Harley. We've got a true emergency on our hands. Hilda needs my help."

"Maybe she does, but the *police* do not need your help. They'll get it sorted out soon enough. You need to stay out of their way. Okay?"

I nodded, but I was thinking: Those two detectives need all the help they can get.

Harley's cell phone started jingling, which spared me from further lectures for the moment.

"I'd better take this. It's the store."

He answered and almost immediately started saying, "Uh-oh," over and over as his face folded into a frown. I swear, Harley's employees can't do anything right if he's not there to watch them. He's too soft-hearted to fire anybody, so he ends up with an entire staff of "Uh-oh's."

I dialed Hilda on my own phone. The call went straight to voicemail, so I left a message telling her about the cable news. I put my phone away and got out a compact and touched up my mascara while Harley finished.

He snapped his phone shut and stomped around the room, loud enough that I pitied whoever was staying below us.

"What's happened now?"

"Bill Hickenlooper backed the forklift into a post in that open-sided shed behind the store."

"Oh, no. Did he break the forklift? That thing cost a fortune."

"Worse. It cracked the steel post."

"How big of a crack?"

Harley took a deep breath, trying to calm himself. It didn't seem to help.

"Doesn't really matter, Loretta. The post holds up one corner of the shed. Any kind of crack, and the whole roof could come down. On top of about a hundred thousand dollars worth of lumber and plywood."

"Oh, my. What'll we do?"

Harley looked around the hotel room, and I could tell he was mentally packing.

"I've got to get back there," he confirmed. "We've got to brace up that roof so we can repair the post or replace it or whatever. I'll see if Stan Lybrand has a welding crew he can spare. And I'll call Ollie over at State Farm, get him working on an insurance claim."

"Can't your people handle this stuff?"

"My people are the ones who broke the shed."

"I don't know why you let Bill Hickenlooper drive that forklift anyway. The man has been completely cross-eyed since the day he was born. His depth-perception has never--"

"Loretta? Not now, hon. I'm trying to think."

I clamped my mouth shut. A little steamed, to tell the truth. But I knew Harley was upset about the accident, so I immediately forgave him.

He stared at the floor, the way he does when the wheels are turning, and I'm sure he was working out the logistics of propping up that roof and fixing that post and firing Bill Hickenlooper once and for all.

Then Harley snapped back to the present and looked straight at me.

"I'm sorry about the film festival, Loretta. But we've got to go home."

"Oh, Harley."

"I know you're disappointed--"

"I'm not going anywhere."

He went sort of goggle-eyed.

"I'm sorry, but I'm needed here. I can't help you at KIMBALLS, but I can help Hilda. She's at the end of her rope already, and the news media is about to set the rope on fire."

"But--"

"You'll be at the store around the clock until the problem is solved. What am I supposed to do? Sit home and make sandwiches?"

He grinned. "You do make a mean sandwich."

"I'll help you pack, and you can head home right away, assuming you can figure out what the valet did with our truck."

A bigger grin.

"You've been a good sport, Harley. You escorted me down the red carpet. You wore your tuxedo. Now you're free to go. The rest of the film festival -- assuming they don't cancel it -- is sitting in dark theaters and listening to speeches and other stuff that would bore you to tears anyway."

I gave him a hug and a peck on the cheek.

"The festival is already paid for. The room is reserved. If I can help Hilda, then it's my duty as fan club president to pitch in."

Perhaps I was overselling it. Worry clouded his face.

"I don't want you to get arrested, Loretta."

"I know. The publicity would be bad for business."

"*Also*, it could be dangerous. It's possible there's a killer staying at this hotel. Did you think about that?"

I hadn't, frankly. I was so worried about the tabloid splash and what it might do to Mr. Girard's career, I'd sort of overlooked the whole murderer-among-us possibility.

"The hotel is full of police. It'll be the safest place in town."

His phone rang. He sighed.

"I'll start packing your stuff," I said.

Ring.

"If I take the Suburban, how will you get home? I may not be able to get away to come get you."

Ring.

"We'll figure it out later." I swallowed, and added: "If I have to, I can catch a ride home with Mitzi."

FAN FAIR: THE OFFICIAL WEBSITE OF THE
INTERNATIONAL MICHAEL GIRARD FAN CLUB
1:22 p.m. March 25

From the President:

By now, I'm sure you've all heard the news reports
erupting from the film festival here in Santa Fe, NM. I am
currently "on the scene," trying to get to the bottom of the
allegations. But I'm sure I speak for all of us when I say there's
simply no way Mr. Girard had anything to do with the death of
Maria Mondragon.

Michael Girard is, above all, a gentleman. Yes, he's a
great actor, but he's never let that go to his head. Throughout his
illustrious career, he's been known as a caring, thoughtful man
who is kind to others. When his wife, Lillian, wasted away with
her long illness, Mr. Girard turned down many potentially
rewarding roles to stay by her side. Their relationship -- thirty
years together with never a hint of scandal -- was considered a
model marriage among Hollywood's elite.

But that's not what's valued these days. All people want
now is gossip and innuendo and filth. Drugs and tattoos and
eating disorders and dramatic breakups and stints in rehab. The
bad apples get all the attention. Not an actor who quietly goes
about his craft, bringing dignity and sophistication to his roles,
one who lives a *normal* off-screen life.

So now, the news media has gone crazy, hounding Mr. Girard and dogging the police and repeating each other's lies. The facts will come out in time, and these so-called journalists will feel bad when it turns out Mr. Girard had nothing to do with the death of that girl, bless her heart. But will they take responsibility? Do you think they'll say, "Oh, sorry. Mr. Girard really had nothing to do with her death, and we slandered him for no good reason." No, they will not. They'll be too busy chasing after the next scandal.

I can assure all of you, the True Fans, that your faith in Mr. Girard is not misplaced. He will weather this storm, just as he has weathered bad reviews and lackluster filmmaking and Lillian's long illness. Mr. Girard will emerge from this mess with his head held high. And we will all be proud that we stood by him.

Sincerely,
Loretta Kimball, president, IMGFC

Chapter 15

Once Harley was on his way, I took the elevator to the penthouse floor. Hilda still wasn't answering her phone, and I was worried about her.

The doors slid open to reveal Officer Can-I-Buy-a-Vowelski standing in the way. (Why do men insist on standing in doorways? You'd think they were all expecting earthquakes.) The cop's face twisted into a scowl at the sight of me.

"Whoops," I said. "Wrong button."

I gave him a little wave to show I had no intention of stepping off that elevator, but he stood glowering while we both waited for the doors to slide shut. It took forever, so I made the most of the moment and stood on tiptoe so I could see past Officer Kielbasa's shoulder.

Except for police, the corridor had emptied, and there was no sign of Hilda. The only civilian I could see was Ava Andrews, who was deep in conversation with Detective Nelson Boyd halfway down the hall. She wore a slinky beige dressing gown, though it was lunchtime, and her hair was freshly brushed. She was an absolute goddess next to Boyd, who looked like a thumb.

I wondered what she might be telling him, but there was no way to pursue it before the elevator started down.

My half-baked plan was to search the lobby for Hilda Schmidt, then go over to the Zia Theater to see if she'd gone there. If I still couldn't find her, I'd return to the hotel coffee shop and get some lunch. I hadn't eaten breakfast because I was too nervous about my interview with Mr. Girard, and now my stomach grumbled like a sleepy teen-ager at dawn. If I stuck close to the hotel, sooner or later I'd run into Hilda.

I came off the elevator, sidestepped a three-foot-tall rubber tree (who thought *those* went with a Southwestern decor, anyway?) and turned a corner. I spotted Mitzi Tyner across the way, and she saw me at the same moment. I again wished I'd worn something less obvious than a stoplight-red blazer.

Mitzi was the usual fashion disaster. Her jacket and long skirt appeared to be made of striped horse blankets, and she wore pointy red boots and enough dripping silver to supply everyone in the hotel with second-place medals. Her black-as-sin hair was teased up and lacquered into place with so much hairspray, she could've been a televangelist.

She was followed by an entourage of gaping admirers, led by Nannette Hoch. Nannette had changed into a blue feed-sack today, and her skinny legs disappeared into battered cowboy boots that came nearly to her knees. She appeared to have slept with curlers on only one side of her head. The other side was flat as the Dead Sea.

I was putting together a wisecrack about holy rollers, but before I could say anything, Nannette pointed at me and said, "*There* she is!"

My first reaction was to run for it, which was odd, considering I had nothing to fear and certainly had done nothing wrong. But I didn't like that accusing finger. Nannette Hoch's the sort of sanctimonious psycho who's always on the lookout for heretics and free thinkers. Her highest ambition in life is to lead an angry mob.

"Loretta! We've been looking all over for you!"

Mitzi and her posse galloped toward me, and there was no escape unless I was willing to hurtle that rubber tree. Backward.

"Hello, Mitzi," I said. "I see you brought your minions."

(I didn't worry about insulting Nannette and the five others with Mitzi. Nannette has hated me since elementary school, and nothing I could say or do would change that situation. The others seemed too young/beautiful/dumb to take offense. Their SPF numbers were higher than their IQs.)

"We heard what happened!" Mitzi said, barging right ahead as if I'd said nothing. "Did Mr. Girard kill that girl?"

I winced. "Do you want to keep your voice down?"

"What's wrong? It's not like it's a big secret--"

"Have you seen Hilda?" I cut in. "Mr. Girard's assistant?"

131

"No." She looked around the group. The minions looked bewildered. "We haven't seen her."

Mitzi stepped closer, and you might've thought that would mean a whisper was coming, but whispering is not her style.

"Were you up there? What did you see? Did you see the corpse? You know how dead bodies creep me out."

She said this last to Nannette, who nodded knowingly, as if they regularly discussed their feelings about the dead.

"There is nothing to fear," Nannette said. "Once the soul has departed, the body is but rancid meat."

I didn't want her to start preaching, so I said, "Okay, okay. If you will hush, I'll tell you what little bit I know."

They eagerly crowded around me, and I kept my voice low as I said, "Maria Mondragon, that intern with the film commission, is indeed dead--"

A little gasp from the minions, as if this was news to them. Maybe everything was news to them.

"--and the police are investigating. But there's no word yet on whether it was an accident or how it happened."

"I heard," said a young man with Buddy Holly glasses, "that Michael Girard was arrested."

"No one has been arrested, as far as I know. They're talking to everyone on the penthouse floor."

More murmuring from the morons. They were already fingering their phones, itchy to send this "inside info" to all their friends.

"So," Mitzi said, "guess you didn't get your interview with Michael Girard, huh? That must be disappointing."

"We're rescheduling it. I've got to firm up a time. That's one reason I'm looking for Hilda."

"We were just headed to the theater," Mitzi said. "Maybe she's over there. Why don't you come with us?"

She made it seem a pleasant suggestion, not a way for her to keep an eye on me. I had a few suggestions for her, most of which involved sharp implements, but what I said was, "I've got to get some lunch. I haven't eaten today."

She laughed merrily, as if my hunger was her favorite joke, then said, "Okay, but you'd better eat fast. Film festival activities resume at two."

"They're going ahead with it, huh?"

"That's what we hear," Mitzi said. "You'd better hurry."

She waved and sailed away, admirers bobbing in her wake.

Chapter 16

I took another circuit of the lobby (still no Hilda), then ordered a salad in the coffee shop because I thought it would be the fastest thing on the menu. Apparently, I was wrong about that. Apparently, for *twelve dollars*, you get an organic salad that's grown fresh from seeds the moment you order it. Before the tiny greens mature, they are plucked from the earth by the tender hands of infants, then delivered by armored car to a chef who artfully arranges them on your plate in a sunset pattern that's ruined as soon as you take one bite.

That's Santa Fe for you.

By the time my snooty waiter delivered the extremely decorative salad and a chunk of hard bread, I was hungry enough to eat the tablecloth. I wolfed down half the roughage without coming up for air, pausing only when my phone rang.

"Mmpf?"

"Loretta, it's Inez. I just heard the news. Are you all right?"

I choked down the mouthful and said, "I'm fine, if still a little shaken up by all this. But my interview with Mr. Girard is on hold for the moment."

"Too bad. I know you were looking forward to it."

"That's the least of our problems now. Every snarky reporter in the country is coming here to make a mockery of Mr.

Girard. Until the police announce that they've cleared his name, it will be a free-for-all around here."

"So he didn't kill anybody?"

"Of course not! Mr. Girard would never do such a thing! God, Inez, you're as bad as the TV people."

My voice had risen, and I looked around the coffee shop. No other diners were looking my way, and the waiters ignored people for a living, so all was clear. Still, I kept my voice down as I added, "Harley's got an emergency at the store, so he just took off for Pandora."

"You're there by yourself?"

"Don't sound so surprised. I can take care of myself perfectly well, thank you."

"That's not what I meant. Harley was supposed to keep an eye on you, remember? Make you behave yourself?"

"Oh, Inez. When has Harley ever gotten me to *behave*? I know how to conduct myself in public. I don't know why you all act like I'm some sort of crazy woman."

A pause, then she said, "Need I remind you that you spent four hundred dollars on a thirty-year-old photograph of Michael Girard in a swimsuit?"

"That was for the archives! And it was a one-of-a-kind picture. I couldn't let an opportunity like that go by--"

"It wasn't even in color!"

"Don't worry about me, Inez. I'll behave. I won't let my lifelong affection for Mr. Girard go to my head."

"Should you even be anywhere near him right now? When the whole world is watching?"

"I've got nothing to hide."

"You have to watch out for gossip, Loretta. That stuff can get on you."

"Only if you make a splash."

Chapter 17

I managed to drip vinaigrette on my jeans. While I waited for my waiter to overcome his ennui and bring my check, I busied myself with trying to get out the stain. I must've been quite a sight, scrubbing at my crotch with a dampened napkin, but I sort of forgot myself because my brain was abuzz with thoughts of murder and gossip and Mr. Girard.

I signed the lunch tab to my room rather than wait for my waiter to complete a correspondence course in how to work the MasterCard machine, and gathered up my purse and went around the corner to the hotel lobby. Other than a few people in line at the front desk, the lobby was mostly empty now, and I guessed that most guests were at the theater already. Maybe Hilda Schmidt was there, too. I checked my wristwatch. Five minutes until two. Good thing I was wearing flats.

As I passed the front desk, I spotted Sean Hyde, the bearded director who was Kip Kaplin's protégé. He was dressed as sloppily as before, baseball cap and all, and his satin jacket had the words "Zombie Picnic" scrolled across the back. Another of his film credits, I suppose.

I veered toward him and said, "Hey, are you checking out?"

He looked at me with bleary eyes, and it took a moment for him to recognize me.

"Yeah. I've got to get back to L.A."

"I thought you guys were here for the whole festival, talking up your Western."

"Yeah, well." Hyde looked away, then back. "That doesn't look so good now, does it?"

"Nonsense. The film festival is going forward. As soon as Mr. Girard emerges from this mess, and that shouldn't take long, he'll be ready to take on some new projects."

"Maybe. But he doesn't seem interested in doing 'Thunder Canyon.'"

"I've always thought he would be so good in a Western, but he's never done one. Of course, I think he's wonderful in everything he does. I'm his biggest fan."

Hyde looked embarrassed, as if everyone were watching us. He tried to sink deeper into the camouflage of his bushy beard.

"Anyway," I said, "it's a shame you're leaving. Is Kip going, too?"

"No, he's staying. At least for now. I don't see the point, but whatever."

I got the feeling Sean Hyde couldn't see the point of much of anything. I can't stand that sort of pessimism, when the world is such a wonderful place with so much to offer. I cheerfully wished him well. He seemed relieved to see me go.

Outside, the sun was bright, but the breeze was chilly. I shivered as I hurried along the sidewalk to the Zia Theater.

The ornate lobby was empty, except for the servers in the concession stand and the ushers at the doors. I slipped inside the dark theater and stopped, waiting for my eyes to adjust.

A spotlight splashed onto the stage, and Andre de Carlo entered from the wings, still dressed in his cowboy fringe. He looked pale and drawn, and he was subdued when he spoke into a cordless microphone.

"Welcome, everyone, welcome, to our matinee screening."

A smattering of clapping, but Andre uncharacteristically kept talking rather than pause for applause.

"As you've no doubt heard by now, our little film festival has been stricken by tragedy. Our thoughts are with the friends and family of Maria Mondragon."

More applause, mostly to cover up the gossiping and whispering in the audience. The theater was only half-full, but I remained standing in the back, scanning the scattered crowd. Searching for Hilda, but also alert for Mitzi and her posse. I didn't want to get roped into sitting with them.

"The police have asked me to say nothing more about her death at this time," Andre said, "and I will abide by their wishes."

I wondered when he'd had that conversation with the police. The only thing I'd heard them tell him was to put down the potted plant and get lost.

Andre sounded strange, speaking lower and slower than usual, as if reading from an unfamiliar script. I wondered if Tony had slipped him a Xanax.

"Despite this terrible blow," Andre said, "we feel it would be in everyone's best interests to continue with the film festival. This afternoon's main event is a screening of the heart-warming classic, 'Hell's Britches,' starring Michael Girard, Evelyn Woodruff and the adorable child star, Squeaky Ackerman. We'd hoped to have Mr. Girard make a few remarks about the film, but he is unable to be with us at this time."

Disappointed "awws" from the audience, along with a few quick boos.

Andre exited stage right, and the maroon curtains parted to reveal a blank movie screen.

Nothing happened for maybe a minute, long enough that people started shifting in their chairs and whispering. Someone backstage (might've been Andre) shouted, "Oh, for shit's sake!" That got a titter from the assembled, then a projector clattered to life and the audio squawked into a swelling of strings.

The screen filled with a familiar landscape, the mountaintop homestead where most of the movie occurs. I've probably seen that film a dozen times, but I still found myself captivated by the screen, especially when the camera zoomed in on a shirtless Mr. Girard splitting wood with an ax. Hard to tear my eyes away, but I had to find Hilda.

I walked down the center aisle, as if headed to a seat in front, but I was checking the faces tilted up to the light of the silver screen. No sign of Hilda, but I did see a few familiar faces, including the matching matadors and the woman with the Big Bird hair. The girl who'd been dressed in spools of film at the gala now wore a gown made from old movie posters. (Such creativity! Wasted on nonsense.)

People began to shift and clear their throats, impatient for me to sit. I went back up the aisle, looking at faces. Halfway to the exit, my phone began to play "Happy Days Are Here Again." I frantically dug it out of my purse, hurrying toward the lobby the whole time.

"Hello?" I kept my voice to a whisper, but was immediately shushed. People can be so rude. "Hold on."

As I went through the swinging doors into the lobby, a tremulous voice came over the phone. "Loretta? It's me. Hilda."

"I've been looking all over for you," I said. "Are you all right?"

"Yeah, I'm, uh, hold on."

Silence. Sunshine streamed through the glass doors and made big yellow squares on the patterned carpet. I stood in one of the warm sunbeams.

"Sorry, Loretta. I'm trying to field a dozen calls at the same time."

"You poor thing. How can I help?"

"Are you here in the hotel?"

141

"I'm at the theater. But I can be back there in a flash."

"I'll meet you in the lobby. There's something I want to tell you, but I don't want to talk about it over the phone."

How tantalizing was *that*? My feet barely touched the ground as I flew back to the Hotel Kokopelli.

Chapter 18

Hilda Schmidt looked terrible. Her face was splotchy, her eyes were bloodshot and her nose was red. Her brittle hair looked like a bundle of kindling.

"Oh, you poor darling," I said as I scooped her up in a hug. "Are you all right?"

She nodded, but she seemed distracted, looking around the airy lobby. People loitered here and there, but no one appeared to be watching us.

"What is it, Hilda? What's going on?"

She shook her head and, clutching my sleeve, led me back out into the bright sunshine.

"The place is already crawling with reporters," she said. "I don't want anyone to hear."

"Of course. Where would you like to go?"

She pointed south, and we strolled along the sidewalk, arm in arm. I asked her about Mr. Girard, and she said he was resting.

"The police really put him through the wringer," she said. "He's exhausted and worried. They moved him down the hall and put a cop outside the door to keep fans and reporters away. Mr. Girard feels like he's under house arrest."

I barely moved my lips as I said, "They don't really believe he had something to do with that girl's death, do they?"

"They're trying to look thorough. The whole world's watching."

The breeze had let up, but we both were shivering as we reached a grassy area along the Santa Fe River. In most places, the rocky-bottomed "river" would be a "ditch" or, at best, a "creek," but water's so scarce here in New Mexico, we make a big deal of every rivulet. A landscaped trail followed the burbling river, winding between barren cottonwoods.

Hilda and I sat on a wooden bench, so close we were cheek-to-cheek, trying to stay warm.

"I think you can help me," she said. "Help Mr. Girard, I mean."

"Whatever you need, sweetie."

"We're putting out a short statement to the press. Mr. Girard is giving no interviews."

I felt crestfallen, but I tried not to let it show.

"But he still wants to do the interview with you."

That propped my crest right back up again. "He does?"

"He said he saw you today. In his suite?"

"Just for a second. Before the detectives ran me off."

"He suggested that the fan club website would be a good place to get a fuller story out."

My face must've flushed as bright red as my jacket. I felt so warm all over, I wondered if I'd suddenly acquired hot flashes. Hilda didn't seem to notice.

"If he goes on TV," she said, "they'll try to trip him up and make him look bad. But you wouldn't do that."

"Of course not!"

"I'll have to run the finished product past the lawyers to make sure nothing accidentally implicates Mr. Girard."

"I'd never want to do anything to harm Mr. Girard."

She patted my arm. "I know, Lorettta. We can rely on you."

"Absolutely. When does he want to do the interview?"

"We're waiting for the okay from his attorney," Hilda said. "So it probably won't be today. Maybe first thing in the morning."

"I'm available whenever he's ready," I said. "My husband got summoned back home -- little emergency at our hardware store -- so I'm Mr. Girard's whenever he wants me."

That didn't come out right, and I got embarrassed, but Hilda was staring at the water tumbling over the rocks.

"You look pale, sweetie. Have you had anything to eat all day?"

She frowned and pressed her hands to her stomach, as if the thought of food was enough to make her sing biscuits.

"Queasy?" I started digging in my purse for antacids. "It's all the stress."

"All the vodka," she muttered.

"Oh, did you drink too much last night?"

"I'm not accustomed to drinking at all."

I found a couple of Pepto-Bismol tablets in the bottom of my purse. They'd been in there a while, but the packaging was intact, and I handed them over. She chewed them slowly.

"What exactly happened after the gala last night, Hilda?"

She looked away. "I told you before."

"You told me Mr. Girard went to bed, but you didn't tell me what *you* did."

"I had a few drinks with some people after Mr. Girard turned in, and then I went to bed myself."

"This at one of those noisy penthouse parties you mentioned earlier?"

Her eyes narrowed. "Just a few people chatting and drinking. A chance to let my hair down. I don't get that very often."

"No big deal then," I said.

"No."

"Is that what you told the police?"

She dropped her gaze to her fidgety hands. "No. I told them I went right to sleep. Mr. Girard really did go straight to bed. I thought it would look better if I'd done the same."

"Someone else at this party will mention that you were there. Then what will you tell the police?"

"Nobody will say anything." She abruptly stood. "I shouldn't have said anything to you."

"You can trust me, Hilda."

"Oh, I know that." She rested a hand on my shoulder. "I'm sorry. I'm all strung out. No sleep. All this stress."

I patted her icy hand, then stood, too. We needed to get indoors before she froze to death.

"Did something happen at that party?" I asked. "Something that needs to be hushed up?"

"No, nothing like that. It's just--"

She looked toward the hotel, then back at me.

"If I tell you something, will you keep it a secret? It'll explain everything."

"Sure, go ahead."

"Promise?"

I did a little cross-my-heart gesture to get her talking. She leaned closer and said, "I was partying with those guys down the hall. Kip Kaplin and Sean Hyde."

That surprised me, but I covered well. "No reason to keep that a secret."

"I've been pushing Mr. Girard to do 'Thunder Canyon.' If he found out I was partying with them, he'd be upset."

We started walking back toward the hotel.

"I saw Sean Hyde a little while ago," I said. "He was checking out, on his way back to L.A. He gave me the impression they were giving up on landing Mr. Girard."

"Kip will *never* give up. But Mr. Girard's just as stubborn. Once he's decided against a project, that's it."

"He seems a very strong-minded man."

147

"This time, he's making a mistake," she said. "I've seen the script. It's terrific."

"They showed it to you?"

"Yesterday, though Mr. Girard doesn't know that. Maria read it, too. That's why she was interested in helping them make the movie in New Mexico. She recognized its quality."

"But Mr. Girard doesn't see it?"

"He just says it isn't right for him. I think it's exactly what his career needs. Maria thought so, too."

"I wonder if that's what she was talking to him about at the gala."

Hilda missed a step, nearly tripped on the brick sidewalk. I caught her skinny arm to keep her from falling.

"You saw Maria talking to Mr. Girard?"

"Backstage. They seemed very cozy."

Hilda frowned. "She tried to sweet-talk him into taking another look at that script. But he wasn't having it."

"Maybe she went to his room later to give it one last shot."

"He says he never saw her after the gala."

We walked in silence for a moment, dodging a trio of slow-moving window-shoppers. The hotel was in the next block, and I had an ugly thought I wanted to broach before we got there. I touched Hilda's arm to stop her.

"Is there any chance that Kip *sent* Maria to Mr. Girard's room? Maybe his little party was a way to keep you busy while the real persuasion went on inside that suite."

Hilda blanched. "You know Mr. Girard better than that. He hasn't *looked* at another woman since his wife died."

"Maria was so young and pretty. That would be enough to make most men kick over the traces."

"Not Mr. Girard."

Chapter 19

Hilda and I parted company in the lobby, amid a growing horde of yammering idiots. She ran off to make more phone calls, and I escaped to my room to freshen up.

The wind had played whoop with my hair, and my eye makeup was smudged. Also, I had a speck of black pepper stuck between my front teeth. How long had *that* been there?

I gave myself a final check in the mirror, then headed back downstairs. I'd just reached the elevators when the bell dinged. Doors slid open to reveal Roger Sherwood (that rat) alone inside.

Most people would be excited and delighted to share an elevator with a real live celebrity, and I'm sure I would've been a dithering fan if it had been anyone else. But Roger Sherwood (that rat) remains the sworn enemy of all fans of Mr. Girard. Our idol's career reached its pinnacle (so far!) when he starred in the first two seasons of "Empire" with Ava Andrews. With his urbane manner, Mr. Girard was perfect as the wise patriarch of the wealthy Greenhalt family. The prime-time soap opera took a turn for the tawdry once he was abruptly replaced. (Of course, the *ratings* went higher as the series got worse. That's the American public for you.)

Today, Roger Sherwood (that rat) was dressed like a bum in ratty jeans and one of those tacky gray sweatshirts that people call hoodies. He had a baseball cap in one hand and a pair of black sunglasses in the other. His hair looked perfect, but he clearly had not shaved this morning.

I gave him a curt nod, then stood facing the elevator doors. My head swam with all the nasty things I'd wanted to say to him over the years, but now that I had my chance, I felt restrained by good manners. I wouldn't fawn over him like so many would, but I couldn't be rude, either.

Big stars can't *stand* to be ignored, of course. He cleared his throat so I'd look over at him, then gave me his patented billboard grin.

"My disguise," he said, brandishing the cap. "Lots of reporters in the lobby. I'd rather not spend the next couple of hours saying, 'No comment.' So I'm forced to sneak out of the hotel."

I barely trusted myself to speak in a civil tone, but I managed to say, "Fame must be a trial."

Again with the impish grin, as if I'd seen right through him and he didn't care. He put the cap on his head, then pulled the gray hood up over it. Before he fitted the sunglasses on, he gave me a wink, making me a co-conspirator in his little subterfuge.

The elevator sighed to a stop at the lobby, and the doors opened onto a mob of TV cameramen and *paparazzi*. The number had doubled while I was upstairs, and their clamor had tripled. Most were dressed for safari, in jeans and boots and multi-pocketed vests, but they acted like a pack of baying dogs. No wonder my fellow passenger needed a disguise.

I turned left as I stepped off the elevator, and began to fight my way to the front door. Roger Sherwood (that rat) went the other way. Before he could get far, I elbowed the nearest cameraman and shouted, "Hey! Isn't that *Roger Sherwood*?"

The cameraman's head whipped around, along with every other head in the vicinity, zeroing in on the man in the Unabomber hoodie. The actor tried to hurry away, but two photographers sprang into his path. The newshounds pressed around him, shouting questions about "Empire" and murder and Michael Girard.

My path to the door cleared, I sailed across the lobby. That same smiling bellhop held the door open for me.

The sunny sidewalks were crowded with shoppers and strollers and amblers, all in my way. Traffic in the street was bumper to bumper. Would I make it to the theater in time to see *any* of Ava Andrews' presentation?

I elbowed my way through the tourists until I reached the T-shaped intersection in front of the Zia Theater. While I waited for a gap in the traffic, I got a weird tingly feeling, and the hair on the back of my neck stood up. Ever get a feeling like that? When you are absolutely certain you are being watched?

I whirled around, but none of the window-shoppers seemed to be paying the least attention to me. I stood on tiptoes to see past them, and caught a glimpse of striped horse blankets vanishing around the corner at the far end of the block.

Why would Mitzi be following me? And, if she *wasn't* following me, why did she try to hide when I turned to see? I checked my wristwatch and sighed. I'd hate to miss Ava Andrews, but I needed to find out what Mitzi was up to now.

I would've felt foolish if I'd reached the corner and found nothing. But no, there were Mitzi and Nannette Hoch, huddled against an adobe wall, whispering like a couple of spies.

"Hey."

They both nearly jumped out of their cowgirl boots.

"Are you two following me?"

"Following you?" Mitzi laughed merrily, but she and Nannette blushed furiously. "Oh, Loretta, you say the craziest things!"

I gave them a level look, but nothing more was forthcoming. "I thought you two went to see 'Hell's Britches.'"

"Why, we did! Didn't we, Nannette?"

Nannette said nothing. Just stared at me malevolently.

"The film ended and we were taking a little walk before the next event. Right, Nannette?"

Still nothing. Nannette was too churchy to lie, but she'd stand by while her idol tried to wriggle her way out of the truth. Mitzi babbled about how much they enjoyed the movie and how wonderful Mr. Girard had looked at that age, but I could tell her mouth was on autopilot. Her scheming brain was busy with something else.

I considered quizzing her on the ending of film (which I could *recite*, I've seen it so many times), but frankly, my dears, I didn't give a damn. Why should I care if the Poodles ducked out in the middle of a classic film? But it was another thing if they were stalking me, trying to weasel their way into my encounters with celebrity.

"You weren't following me?"

"No, silly. We were just window-shopping for a few minutes before Ava Andrews takes the stage. Speaking of which, we'd better hurry back there, don't you think?"

She made a big show of looking at her watch, then she and Nannette scurried toward the theater, casting nervous glances back at me.

Hmm. They were up to something. I felt sure it would turn out to be something stupid and loud and humiliating. I briefly wished I could pack them in a big box and ship them back to Pandora.

Air holes optional.

Chapter 20

The ushers frowned at me as I hustled across the carpeted lobby of the Zia Theater. Don't know why they felt that was necessary; someone has to be last to arrive, and it's not *always* me, I'm sure.

I pushed through the heavy swinging doors into the darkened theater, and involuntarily said, "Whoa."

Every seat was occupied, and the carpeted aisles were crowded with enough photographers to give a fire marshal a heart attack. The air was thick with the aromas of popcorn and perfume and perspiration.

Ava Andrews sat on a tall stool on stage, basking in the glow of a spotlight. She wore a broomstick skirt and a loose tunic with a geometric pattern woven into the bodice. On her, Santa Fe style looked chic, whereas on Mitzi it seemed one more in a long line of frauds. Of course, someone as naturally glamorous as Ava Andrews could wear a burlap bag and get away with it. She smiled into her microphone and said, "And *that* was the first time I ever met Michael Girard."

The audience erupted into laughter and applause, making me sorry I'd missed that anecdote. Yet another thing to blame on Mitzi and Nannette.

As my eyes adjusted, I saw Tony Lodge standing against the back wall of the theater. He still wore his cowboy duds, but he'd ditched the hat, which seemed a wise fashion decision. He cocked an eyebrow, clearly recognizing me from our earlier eviction. I gave him my most winning smile, and it cracked his shell a little. He waved me over.

"No more seats," he whispered. "Sorry."

"That's okay."

We faced forward as Ava Andrews resumed her remarks.

"I loved working with Michael the first two seasons," she said. "And I adored Roger, of course. But the series got to be a grind over nine years. After 'Empire' was canceled, I'd had enough of that pace. And, frankly, I'd had enough of Hollywood. I moved here to Santa Fe."

A smattering of applause from the locals made her beam.

"I've always loved this magical place. And the people here made me feel right at home."

More applause.

"It helped, of course, that I met my husband here," she said. "Santa Fe is a wonderful place for a courtship, I can tell you that. A very romantic city!"

Oh, the crowd ate that up with a spoon! No one applauded louder than Tony, who seemed relieved that something was going right for change.

Ava Andrews asked her husband to stand up and take a bow. For once, the spotlight operators were awake, and they found him in the audience. He was a stork-like older man who waved a Stetson over his head as if he could catch applause in it. He reminded me of Mitzi's husband back in Pandora. I wondered if he was rich like Long John Tyner, and if that was what the actress saw in him.

"And now," she said, "I'd like to bring out the man who made this entire film festival possible -- Andre de Carlo!"

Oh, that made Tony pound his hands together harder than ever! The rest of the audience seemed a little less enthusiastic, but the SFSSSFF *was* off to a rocky start and we weren't ready to throw roses at Andre yet.

He'd made yet another costume change, one that reflected a more somber mood. His black suit was perfectly tailored, and he wore a white shirt open at the collar. He looked positively manly, in fact, except for his high-heeled boots.

Tony was the last one to stop clapping. He stared at Andre with so much love in his eyes, it made me miss Harley.

Ava Andrews slid off her stool to give Andre a hug, then she said into her microphone: "Andre, I think it's time you come out of the closet--"

A gasp rippled through the audience.

"--and reveal to everyone that you are secretly my little brother."

Andre's face split into a smile. She handed over the microphone, but he had to wait for the applause to die down before he could say anything.

"Thank you, thank you. Okay, it's true. I'm a lucky, lucky man to have a famous actress for a big sister."

I was as surprised as the rest of the applauding audience. I leaned over and said into Tony's ear, "His sister? Really?"

"He was born *Carl Andrews*." Tony rolled his eyes, as if no name had ever fit anyone worse.

Andre de Carlo put his arm around his sister. Side by side like that, there definitely was a family resemblance.

"Since I'm *so* much younger than my sister--"

Uneasy laughter. Ava Andrews' gaze went frosty, but her professional smile never wavered.

"--we didn't spend nearly enough time together when I was growing up. But Ava introduced me to Santa Fe a few years ago, and I, too, felt a magical connection with this place."

More hooting and applause. Apparently, they could just stand on stage and say "Santa Fe" over and over, and that would be enough to please this crowd.

"Ava has been invaluable in helping us get this film festival started," Andre said. "In more ways than I can ever describe."

He said this with less enthusiasm than it seemed to warrant, but the audience clapped anyway. My palms were getting chapped.

"They should sell hand lotion at the concession stand," I said to Tony.

"What?"

"Never mind."

Andre apologized to the attendees because the hotel and theater were overrun.

"I know this isn't the festival experience you registered for," he said. "We'll do our best to muddle through, despite the police presence and all the media."

Andre gestured at the *paparazzi* crouching in the aisles, and was rewarded with a blizzard of flashes. Once the cameras stopped chattering, he reminded the audience that the next event would be a showing of "The Meek" (which I've seen so many times, I've lost count), starting in twenty minutes.

"I'm sorry to say Mr. Girard will not be appearing after the screening, as scheduled," Andre said.

More flashes and a chorus of "aww's" from the audience. A few reporters dashed for the exits, presumably to call in this latest update.

"Sorry, sorry," Andre said until everybody piped down. "Mr. Girard's just not feeling up to it, after all that's happened. But let me remind you that we have a full slate of films old and new for tomorrow. We hope he will join us at some point during the day."

The applause seemed half-hearted. I couldn't blame the crowd for feeling disappointed. Without Mr. Girard, the night lost much of its star power.

Andre announced the evening films, which would follow dinner "on your own," but the titles didn't register with me since they didn't feature Mr. Girard. He thanked everyone again, then exited the stage with his sister on his arm.

The house lights came up, and the audience got to its feet, sighing and groaning and stretching. I turned to comment on the big turnout, but Tony had disappeared, so I joined the slow-moving exodus to the exits.

The creeping crowd got me thinking: The bad publicity surrounding Maria Mondragon's death was about the best thing that could've happened to this fledgling film festival.

Chapter 21

Just as fresh air and sunshine seemed within reach, a large woman stopped in the lobby door to answer her cell phone. She was one of those women who carry all their weight in the hips, bless her heart, so it looked like she was smuggling a rubber boat under her skirt. I tried to navigate past her and ran into the sharkskin sports coat of Kip Kaplin. The tightly wound producer jumped at the contact.

"Sorry!" I said. "Trying to *clear* the *door*."

The fat woman went right on with her phone call, oblivious. Some people, I swear.

Kip and I squeaked through a gap and made it out onto the crowded sidewalk. He made a narrower wake than my beloved Harley, but I followed along, smiling and nodding like the Queen Mum.

When we were clear of the throng, Kip immediately lit a cigarette. Between his noxious smoke and the exhaust fumes of passing cars, there wasn't much fresh air to be had, but it still was good to be outdoors. The low sun illuminated puffy clouds. It promised to be the usual glorious New Mexico sunset.

"I'm beat." Kip pushed up his narrow glasses to rub at an eye. "Got up way too early."

"Kind of noisy on the penthouse floor this morning."

"Yeah." He puffed on his cigarette some more, looking away, ready for me to move along.

"And you've probably got a hangover," I said.

"How's that?"

"I hear there was a party in your suite last night." I slipped him a wink. "You tie one on?"

He dropped the cigarette and stomped on it, though it wasn't halfway done. "Who told you that?"

"Hilda claims to have the mother of all hangovers, so I figured you probably had one, too."

"You talked to Hilda."

"I'm helping her with media."

"Uh-huh."

"I ran into your buddy Sean Hyde this morning. He looked like he'd seen better days as well."

Kip stood on his toes to look past me, surveying the crowd for a better networking opportunity.

"He said he was flying back to Los Angeles," I said.

"He thought he was. I talked to him on the phone. He was stuck in the Albuquerque airport."

I made some polite noises about how that was too bad, but Kip cut me off, saying, "Serves him right. He committed to being here the whole weekend. But as soon as things get weird, he splits."

"I imagine he's not the only one," I said. "A lot of folks were checking out."

"Lots more were trying to check in. All this media attention? We could *use* this. But he hauls ass instead."

Before I could pursue that further, a screech sounded right behind me, nearly lifting me off my feet.

"Lo-*retta*!"

The unmistakable call of Mitzi Tyner. Kip pressed his hand to forehead, as if to contain a throb of hangover pain. I knew exactly how he felt, though the pains Mitzi gave me typically were in the derriere region.

"We've been looking all *over* for you!"

Squinting against the shrillness, I said, "I've got to get better at hiding."

Mitzi laughed gaily and slapped me on the shoulder. Nannette glowered beside her like a cat on a leash.

"You must be one of Loretta's *Hollywood* friends!" Mitzi introduced herself and Nannette, and they shook hands all around. Kip's eyes darted back and forth, looking for an escape. I was doing the same.

"We're so excited about all the movies being made in New Mexico now," Mitzi gushed. "Of course, *we've* known all along that this Land of Enchantment is a beautiful place, but it's taken Hollywood to show that to the world."

She insisted that he simply *must* visit Pandora while scouting locations. She started telling him all that Pandora could offer to visiting filmmakers, but after Red Mesa and Route 66, she seemed to run out of points of interest.

He mumbled something about tax incentives, but I didn't catch it. I had taken a step backward, making room for Nannette to close ranks, and saw my opportunity to melt into the crowd at the crosswalk.

Kip had a trapped, pleading expression on his face, but I couldn't help him. I was intent on saving myself.

Chapter 22

I tried to stopper my ears as I moved through the babbling rabble streaming toward the Hotel Kokopelli. The crowd was abuzz with talk of murder and scandal and Mr. Girard, and I could hardly stand it.

"Movie stars think they can get away with anything," said a man just ahead of me. "Somebody will clean up behind them."

I recognized him as he spoke to his girlfriend. They were the black-clad urbanites I'd noticed on opening night. She still wore those weird earrings that looked for all the world like cup hooks.

"He'll get away with it," she sneered. "The cops in this burg probably bribe cheap."

"Oh, why don't you both shut up?" I said, louder than I intended. "You don't know what you're talking about!"

They went bug-eyed at the sudden interruption.

"Mr. Girard would never, ever harm another human being," I said. "He is a gentleman."

"You know Michael Girard?" said a man behind me.

"I do." I turned to find a sawed-off young man in a rumpled linen jacket. "I'll have you know I am president of the International Michael Girard Fan Club, and as such, I know him as well as anyone. So there."

He seemed unaffected by the volume of my devotion. He reached inside his jacket as if going for a gun, and pulled out a notebook.

"Have you talked to Mr. Girard today?"

"Oh, no, you don't. You want a statement about Mr. Girard, you should see his assistant, Hilda Schmidt. I have nothing to say to the likes of you."

He grinned at my feistiness, but the startled urbanites hurried away. Too bad. I had a few more choice words for them.

"Come on, lady," the reporter said. "Stand up for your movie idol. Prove Girard isn't guilty."

"I don't have to prove anything!"

I stormed off, but my exit was ruined when my toe snagged on the uneven sidewalk. People gasped as I nearly went tumbling, but I caught my balance in time. I pulled myself together, ignoring some ill-mannered snickering, and marched off to the hotel in search of Hilda.

Good heavens, what a commotion! The lobby was jammed with barking reporters and elbowing camera crews. It was a "media circus," and they all seemed like clowns to me. We needed a ringmaster to keep order.

I weaved my way across the lobby, occasionally standing on tiptoe to look for Hilda. It's a wonder I found her at all. A dozen newshounds had pinned her in a corner near the Kokopelli fountain, snapping questions and whining for answers. Some held cameras at arms' length above the herd, pointed down at Hilda, who looked battered by the flashbulbs.

"I can't say anything beyond what is in the statement," she said. "There's no point in asking me!"

I tried to push my way through the pack, but they were accustomed to jostling and pushed right back without even looking.

Hilda shrank into her corner, her lip trembling. I knew she'd hate to be captured on camera, weeping. Plus, that wouldn't look good for Mr. Girard. I needed to do something to help.

"Look!" I shrieked. "It's Roger Sherwood!"

The newshounds wheeled, looking to where I pointed. Of course, there was nothing to see, just more reporters, but most of the pack ran over there to make sure.

I grabbed Hilda's skinny arm and dragged her away from the few lingering hacks. She thanked me all the way to the elevator.

Chapter 23

The penthouse floor was no longer sealed off, except for Mr. Girard's former suite, which had yellow "crime scene" tape crisscrossed over the door, and his new room at the far end of the hall, where a uniformed officer stood watch. The sight of that guard made me sad for Mr. Girard. It really did seem as if he were under house arrest.

Once we were inside Hilda's room, she went straight to the bathroom and shut the door. She ran water to cover the noise, but I could tell she was having herself a good cry. Who could blame her? People yelling in her face all day. How awful.

I wandered over to the windows and looked out at the vivid watercolor sky. No place on Earth has sunsets like New Mexico. It's one reason I could never live anywhere else.

I opened the sliding window a few inches to let in some air. No balcony or rail on the big window, which seemed dangerous to me. The upper floors of the Hotel Kokopelli stepped back from the ground floor, pueblo style, but these windows were at the rear of the hotel, and it was a straight drop to the sidewalk five stories below. Looking down gave me the shivers.

Hilda came out of the bathroom, toweling off her face.

"Whew, that's better," she said. "I nearly had a panic attack, trapped in that corner."

"I know, sweetie. They were acting like animals! But it's over now. You can take a minute for yourself. Have you eaten?"

She shook her head. "No time. And no appetite."

"Your body needs calories to burn. You're under a lot of stress."

"You can say that again." She sat on the end of the bed, dabbing at her eyes. "This is more than I bargained for."

She buried her face in the white towel. I've always envied women who can cry quietly. I don't weep often, but when I do, it's hysterical enough to make Harley go outside, even during a blizzard.

"You must've known," I said gently, "when you went to work for a celebrity, that there was always the possibility of something like this. The nation thrives on scandal."

She looked up at me, her eyes redder than ever. "Not with Mr. Girard! He's so, so *good*. You know?"

"I know, dear."

"I don't see how anyone could believe he'd *party* with Maria Mondragon, much less think he was responsible for her death."

"I've been saying the same thing."

"You're such a good friend to him," she said. "He knows it, too. He'll tell you himself when you see him in the morning."

"The interview's still on?"

"Ten o'clock, unless something changes overnight. We might have to juggle it a little, depending on the police and the lawyers."

"Whenever you say," I said. "I'm delighted he'd make the time with all that's going on."

"A fan club interview won't get the media off our backs, but it's a start. I've got to do *something*."

Hilda leaked more tears into the towel. "God, my head is pounding."

I dug in my purse and found two Tylenol that weren't too linty.

"You must think I'm a walking pharmacy," I said as I fetched her some water. "I hardly ever get headaches myself, but my daughter Jessica used to get the worst migraines."

"This is not a migraine," Hilda said glumly. "It's self-inflicted. I almost never touch alcohol. Seems like something bad happens every time I do."

I recalled past telephone conversations about her poor choices in boyfriends. Always met them in bars. Hmm. Not the proper time to share this insight, so I said, "If it's any comfort, you're not the only one who's suffering. Kip Kaplin looks like something the cat dragged in."

She nearly choked, but she got the Tylenol down and said, "You talked to Kip?"

"Little while ago, outside the theater. I told him that partying would be the death of him."

I hadn't said anything of the kind, of course, but I was trying to make her feel better about her own miserable state.

"Did he say anything about me?"

"We didn't really get to talk. We got interrupted by my so-called friends from Pandora."

"That woman Mitzi?"

I nodded. "My cross to bear. But you don't need to hear about her. You need to look after yourself. Let's get you something to eat."

"I can't." Hilda got to her feet. "Not now. I've got to go see Mr. Girard. He's been on the phone with his attorneys all afternoon. I haven't had a chance to talk to him."

She twisted the towel in her hands.

"I've decided to tell him about the party. He's in a lot of trouble. I could be making it worse by lying to the police."

"Lying almost never helps," I said. "But sometimes, in the heat of the moment, we blurt things out. Mr. Girard will understand that. So will the detectives. Just tell them the truth. You'll feel better."

She worried over that for a few seconds, then said, "I'll talk to Mr. Girard first. See what he wants me to do."

"You'll get it straightened out, sweetie. I'm sure of it."

She stood and tucked at her clothes, pulling herself together. She still had the white towel, and I thought it was a good sign when she cast it onto the bed. Maybe her tears were finished. I followed her into the corridor and watched as she

171

made sure her door locked behind us.

"Don't forget to eat," I said.

"I'll get room service with Mr. Girard."

"Good idea. Talking over food always works for Harley and me. Just be sure to hide the steak knives."

That made her laugh a little. Sometimes, a laugh is the very best gift you can give a person.

Hilda straightened her spine and marched off toward the far end of the corridor. I stepped into the elevator and watched her go. She'd just reached the officer outside Mr. Girard's room when the elevator doors slid shut.

Chapter 24

Harley was still at KIMBALLS when I reached him by phone, and he sounded harried and tired. I tried to keep it brief, but so much had happened, it took me a while to catch him up. I told him about Hilda's hangover/nervous breakdown and Mr. Girard's seclusion and the mob in the lobby and Ava Andrews' surprise relationship with Andre de Carlo and the vinaigrette spill on my jeans and my elevator encounter with Roger Sherwood (that rat).

Harley kept saying, "Uh-huh," the way he does on the phone, always sounds like he's writing down your order.

"Anyway," I said, wrapping up, "the biggest news is that my interview with Mr. Girard is on again! Ten o'clock tomorrow morning."

"I thought there was a cop outside his door."

"Hilda's fixing it so I'll be allowed inside."

"Will she be there with you?"

"I assume so. Why?"

"She wants to approve the message before it goes out to the public, right? I'm sure she'll keep you from straying into hazardous areas."

Something in his tone told me there was more.

"I guess I'm perfectly capable of conducting an interview on my own," I said. "I'd never ask Mr. Girard a question that would make him uncomfortable."

A pause.

"I just thought she should be there."

"Why, Harley Kimball! Are you worried about me being alone with Mr. Girard?"

"No, it's just--"

"Because he is always a perfect gentleman."

"I *know*, hon. It's not that. I'm worried about all this media stuff. Don't you feel like these people are *using* you?"

"Oh, they probably are, Harley, but I don't mind. The fans are my first priority, and they're dying for information. They'd never forgive me if I didn't do my best by them during this awful time."

Harley grumped that the fans could watch CNN like everybody else, but I knew he didn't mean it. He's always very understanding about my presidential responsibilities.

"My interview could still be derailed by the police or by Mr. Girard's lawyers."

"Lawyers. This keeps getting worse."

"It's *okay*, Harley. Everyone is making sure that we're helping Mr. Girard and not harming his position. That's all."

He sort of harrumphed, but I knew he was under a lot of stress himself.

"How about you?" I asked. "How are things there?"

"We're going to have to replace that post. And now the forklift's conked out, too."

"Was Bill Hickenlooper driving it?"

"Now, Loretta. The man can't help his vision problems. And no, he won't be driving the forklift anymore. I had Juan moving lumber out of that end of the shed, so the welders would have room to work, and the forklift just died."

"Great."

"Plus, I walked out in the yard to find a whole truckload of low-flow toilets that I did not order sitting on pallets out in the weather."

"Toilets?"

"Some mix-up in shipping. And nobody here snapped to it when they were delivered."

"Can't you store them someplace? Toilets will always sell eventually."

"Not these. They're *pink*."

"Oh, my."

"That's just an annoyance. This repair on the shed is a real emergency. The welders will be working into the night. I don't even want to think how much that's going to cost."

"Insurance will cover it, Harley."

"But that doesn't solve the immediate problem. I've got untreated wood sitting out in the elements, and it looks like rain. And I've got a bunch of welders throwing sparks everywhere in a lumber shed."

"Good heavens. I hope you've got people standing by with fire hoses."

He sighed. "Of course I do, Loretta."

"Don't give a hose to Bill Hickenlooper. He'll just spray himself in the face."

That got him to laugh, which of course was my intent.

"Did you eat anything after that long drive home?" I asked.

"A doughnut. And about six Diet Cokes."

"You know that's not good for your blood sugar, Harley. You need real food to keep you going."

"I'll get something, soon as I can. What about you? Are you headed out to a fancy restaurant?"

"Haven't really made a plan," I said. "Hilda's busy with Mr. Girard. Everyone else, I'm trying avoid. I'll probably just slip out for a burger or something."

"A hamburger? In Santa Fe? Think we can afford that? They'll probably want twenty bucks for it."

"Right. And it'll be made out of free-range yak."

"With tofu on the top."

"Now I'm not hungry anymore."

Harley laughed. He sounded much cheerier than when he answered the phone, so I felt I had done my wifely duty.

"I know you need to get back," I said. "But look after yourself."

"You, too. I don't like being apart overnight like this."

"I know. Hardly ever happens."

"Not since the wild days of your youth."

Harley likes to tease me about the years when I was away at college in Albuquerque. I've told him about my adventures and love affairs from those years, of course; we don't keep secrets from each other. But he likes to pretend my single years were a lot wilder than they were, while he dutifully waited for me to return to Pandora and marry him.

"Well, there were those nights when I traveled with Jessica's softball team," I said. "Pretty wild. Motels. Pillow fights."

"That's right. And you have no idea what Ben and I got up to on those overnight 'fishing' trips."

"I knew you were leading that child astray," I said.

Harley's laugh was interrupted by a crash in the background.

"Oh, hell," he said. "I've got to go."

"I'll call you tomorrow and let you know how it goes with Mr. Girard."

"Be careful with those folks, Loretta."

Another crash.

"Oh, hell."

"Go, go! Good-bye."

Chapter 25

I changed jackets before I went downstairs. I didn't
know what the evening might bring, but my red blazer had
proven a handicap to snooping. I'd packed a lovely gray coat
that would be invisible in the dark. I felt like a spy as I checked
myself in the mirror.

The elevator was jammed on the way down, but I didn't
recognize anyone on board. A few reporters and cameramen
still loitered in the lobby, but the rest had evaporated, no doubt
pumping revenue into the local saloons. The clerks at the front
desk looked like shaken survivors. Their phones rang and rang.

I did a quick circuit around the lobby and coffee shop,
looking for familiar faces, but finding none. Hard to snoop on
people when they weren't around, but I was prepared to broaden
my scope. Also, I needed dinner, and I didn't have half a
lifetime to wait on another hotel salad.

Outside, the air was crisply cold with a hint of faraway
moisture. The clouds had thickened, blanking out the stars. I
said a little prayer that Harley would get his repairs completed
before any rain arrived in Pandora.

I figured restaurants near the plaza would be more
expensive, so I went the opposite direction in search of
sustenance. I didn't need much. A quick sandwich, maybe a
glass of wine to calm my nerves. Then I'd hustle back to the

hotel and see if I could learn how things had gone between Hilda and Mr. Girard.

I walked along the street behind the hotel, looking up at the highest windows, wondering how Mr. Girard was reacting to Hilda's confession. Her lie was a small transgression, one that still could be redeemed. I hoped he would see it that way, too.

I wanted the best for Hilda. She reminded me of myself at that age, though I was never that skinny. I remember how it felt to be that young and trying to make sense of careers and friendships and relationships. Young women can feel so *alone* when they're single and far from home, and that sometimes makes it hard to do the right thing. I was proud of the way Hilda squared up her shoulders and faced her responsibilities.

Maria Mondragon had been another feisty single girl trying to make it in the world. So much potential. It made me sad to think she'd never reach it now.

I turned a corner and went another half a block before I found a cafe with a neon "OPEN" sign. It was a Mexican restaurant called Tortilla Curtain. Mostly empty, and one look at the menu explained why: It was priced for tourists who didn't know any better. I was hungry enough to ignore the costs (monetary and caloric), and I ordered a big platter of spicy, cheesy goodness from a friendly waitress.

I nibbled on chips and sipped my wine while I waited for my meal. Felt like it was the first time I'd sat still all day.

The waitress had curly black hair like Maria Mondragon's, and I shivered at the thought of Maria's head getting caved in.

I still didn't believe for even a second that Mr. Girard had anything to do with her death. She either got into his suite on her own initiative, or somebody *put* her in there.

She could've been drunk, fallen, hit her head. Maybe she dragged herself onto that sofa and expired there. But surely she could've made enough noise to wake Mr. Girard. If I were the one bleeding from the head, I'd wake everybody on the whole floor. Unless she'd been knocked unconscious. But then how did she get on that sofa?

Suppose Maria had been injured (or even died) elsewhere. If you had a corpse on your hands, you could do worse than to dump her in Mr. Girard's suite. People are only too happy to believe the worst about celebrities.

Hmm. That theory had lots of holes in it, too, not the least of which was why someone needed to get rid of a body on the penthouse floor of the Hotel Kokopelli.

My platter of calories arrived, and I dug in, but I hardly tasted the spicy food. I was too busy spinning scenarios in my head.

I was pretty sure Maria died on the penthouse floor. Not very likely that someone would cart a dead or injured woman into the elevator and up to the top floor. Even late at night, that would be risky. So, she was killed or injured up there, then was deposited in Mr. Girard's suite while he slept.

Who else was staying on the penthouse floor? Hilda, of course, a couple of doors away. Kip Kaplin and Sean Hyde were staying on that floor because Hilda had partied with them. What about Andre and Tony? Surely, they hosted one of the parties there; Hilda said they'd reserved the entire floor. I hadn't recognized the other guests I'd seen in the corridor, but maybe they were behind-the-scenes people like Hilda. I felt certain the police were checking all of them for any connection to Maria Mondragon.

I wondered if they questioned Sean Hyde before he left town. The director certainly had seemed in a hurry to get away from Santa Fe.

His buddy Kip reminded me of a boy who'd gone to Pandora High with us. Leon Purdue. He was a skinny, nervous type, always hustling people, trying to make a buck off them. Selling cigarettes right on the school grounds! If he'd been around for senior year, I'm sure he would've been voted "Most Likely to Deal in Used Cars."

Leon is the last person Harley ever hit with his fist. The little weasel was following me down the hall, sniggering with his friends, and he dropped a very bad word that begins with the letter "c."

People might talk that way in the big city, but it's not accepted in Pandora, then or now. Speak like that in the presence of a lady, and a Pandora man feels it is his duty to flatten you. And then make you apologize.

Harley was standing nearby. (When I was in high school, Harley was *always* standing nearby. Sometimes, he even got up the nerve to speak to me.) When he heard what Leon said, Harley didn't hesitate. He took one long step in the smaller boy's direction and planted his fist squarely upside his skull.

Well. It broke Harley's hand, of course. Fortunately, it was not during football season, or Coach Faulkner would still be kicking Harley's butt. But Harley did get suspended from school for a week, and he had to get through final exams with a cast on his writing hand. He likes to say that's why he never went to college, which is total bull, but it tickles him to say it.

Leon never did properly apologize. But he seemed even twitchier after that, and he always minded his manners around me. His family moved away a few months later. I sometimes wonder whatever happened to those people.

Anyway, Kip reminded me of that boy Leon, and I thought it was just as well that Harley had gone home before he spent any more time around him. Harley can't afford another broken hand.

I made a mental note to talk to Kip again. Maybe he saw Maria on the penthouse floor.

I sipped some ice water to cool the burn of the green chile. Whew. Not as spicy as the food at Rosita's Route 66 Cafe in Pandora, but still hot enough to make one perspire around the eyeballs.

Half my meal was gone already, bolted blindly while I was lost in thought. I told myself to slow down. Not often that I dine out alone. I should savor it.

The restaurant was awfully quiet for a Friday night. Candle-lit couples occupied two other tables, but we customers were outnumbered by the staff and that's never a good sign. Probably the location, back here on this dark street. I'll bet the restaurants around the plaza were chock full of tourists and TV reporters.

I finished my meal without any epiphanies, but I did wonder some more about the other guests on the penthouse floor. Why did Ava Andrews need a suite, when she had a home right here in town? Had her long-faced husband spent the night on that floor, too? Had they all partied with Andre and Tony? Had Maria been with them?

I left an extra-large tip for the waitress (partly because she reminded me of Maria), and was headed out the door when I nearly bumped into two men. I sort of yelped in surprise, then I recognized them, and I yelped again. Detectives Nelson Boyd and Rick Torres.

"Aw, Christ," said Boyd, "it's *her* again."

"Well, hello to you, too. Is that the way you greet all the tourists? The Chamber of Commerce must appreciate that."

"Don't talk to me," Boyd said. "You give me a pain."

"I beg your pardon?"

"You heard me."

"That is no way to speak to a lady," I said. "Surely your mother raised you better than that."

Boyd said a word that should never be uttered in polite company, much less in an establishment where people are eating. He stalked to a booth at the far end of the cafe and plunked himself down.

His partner shrugged at me. "It's a been a long day."

"For all of us," I said.

I took a deep breath, remembering that these two idiots likely had tons of useful information.

"How's your investigation going? Making progress?"

Another shrug. "Can't really talk about it."

"I'm not a journalist or anything," I said. "I'm just curious."

"I know who you are."

I didn't appreciate his tone, but I didn't say so.

"I was thinking about something," I said. "I guess the police made a list of everybody staying on the penthouse floor, huh?"

"Of course."

"Any way you could share that information with me? I know who some of the guests are, but I'm--"

I could tell by the way his close-set eyes glazed over that he'd stopped listening.

"Never mind," I said. "Forget I asked. It's none of my business."

"That's right. It's not."

Again, with the tone. Sheriff Johnson back in Pandora would never dream of speaking to me that way, but I guess things are different in the big city.

"Good night, Detective," I said politely. "Enjoy your meal."

I waited until the restaurant door closed completely before I added, in my best movie-moll voice: "Hope you choke on it, copper."

Chapter 26

I walked back the way I'd come. There probably was a more direct route, but I knew better than to take chances with unfamiliar streets. Downtown Santa Fe is a maze. I turned onto the street that ran along the rear of the Hotel Kokopelli, hoping there was a back door I'd overlooked when I was hunting for a restaurant. Even darker on this shadowy street than it had been before. Sort of creepy, in fact, and I walked faster.

The building loomed above the sidewalk like a mud cliff studded with windows. Some were lit from within, and I tipped my head back, trying to see up to the penthouse. I was itching to call Hilda, but decided to check the lobby first, see if she was downstairs. If I couldn't find her, maybe I'd slip a few bucks to a bellhop, see if I could get the names of--

Smack!

Something hit the sidewalk up ahead, so loud my first thought was that some drunk had thrown a chair from a room above. I looked up, searching the windows, but didn't see any dark shapes or hear any crazed laughter. All was as it had been before up there.

A chill ran over me as realization dawned.

That was no chair.

I took a couple of unsteady steps forward, staring at the lumpy bundle on the sidewalk. It was a person all right. Dark jeans and shirt, but I could make out a pale, thin arm. A dead woman. I could tell she was broken all to pieces by the fall. She looked like a bag of elbows.

I leaned closer. Her face was smashed on one side, flattened against the unyielding concrete. The other eye was wide open, looking right at me.

I screamed at the top of my lungs.

It was Hilda Schmidt.

Chapter 27

Before I even thought to dial 911, I heard sirens approaching. I think I'd gone into shock, to tell you the truth. I sort of *found* myself kneeling next to Hilda, my face in my hands.

I didn't touch her. Nothing I could do for her. I only hoped death had come so quickly that she didn't feel the impact.

Feet slapped the sidewalk near me. I wiped at my eyes, and the first thing to come into focus was the bulldog face of Detective Nelson Boyd.

"What happened?" he barked. "Did she fall?"

He leaned back to look up at the windows, same as I had done.

Someone gently clutched my shoulders and helped me to my feet. Detective Torres cradled me in his arms, and I bawled into his shirtfront.

"It's okay, it's okay," he kept saying, but that couldn't possibly be right. Nothing was okay. Hilda lay on the concrete, a pile of broken bones. A black pool oozed from beneath her hair, and it took me a second to recognize it as blood.

Torres turned me away from the horrible sight. Before I could object, he handed me off to the nearest bystander, who took me into a full embrace before I realized it was Mitzi Tyner.

"Oh, you poor thing," she said. "You miserable, unlucky girl. What a terrible thing to witness!"

It says something about the shock of the situation that I didn't jerk away. At a time like this, human contact's the only comfort, even if it came in the form of Mitzi. We hugged each other like we didn't have decades of grudges caked up between us. We must've been quite a sight, boohooing there in the middle of the street while police and paramedics and photographers and rubberneckers filled the block around us with a confusion of noise and flashing lights.

Nannette Hoch stood nearby the whole time but never shed a tear. She was too busy glaring at me like it was my fault some girl went flying to her death. She finally remembered her Christian charity and dug a giant wad of Kleenex out of her purse. She handed the tissues to Mitzi, who split them with me, and we took a minute to pull our faces together and catch our breaths.

I was thankful to see that they'd covered up Hilda's broken-doll body with a white sheet. Detectives Boyd and Torres huddled in conversation just beyond her corpse, and uniformed policemen were "securing the perimeter," as they say on TV, aiming their flashlights in people's faces and ordering them to stay back. A trio of cameramen rounded the far corner of the hotel, throwing more shafts of light into the mix, but the officers greeted them with outstretched arms and shaking heads.

"All these people," I said. "It's like they came out of nowhere."

"You screamed loud enough to wake the dead," Nannette said.

"I was stunned."

"Of course you were, dear," Mitzi said. "It's terrible, terrible. The worst thing I've ever seen. I'm just heartbroken."

Even through my shock and dismay, I bristled a little. We all felt horrible for Hilda, true, but it wasn't *about* how Mitzi felt, was it?

"How did you get here so fast?" I asked. "Were you two *following* me again?"

"No, of course not," Mitzi said, but I could tell she was lying. "We, um, finished dinner and we were going back to the hotel."

"Just like you," Nannette said.

"How do you know I was at dinner? You *were* following me."

"Oh, stop it, Loretta. This is no time to make one of your 'scenes.'"

"What the hell are you ta--"

"Mrs. Kimball?"

I turned at the sound of my name. Detective Torres stood ten feet away, over by Hilda, crooking a finger at me. I sighed.

"I've got to go," I said. "But we're not done with this."

Mitzi touched her tissue to her cheek and said to Nannette, "Pay no attention to her. She's overwrought."

Grrr.

My annoyance at Mitzi burned away some of my grief and shock. By the time the detectives got me off to one side (cornered against some pointy shrubbery), I pretty much had myself under control.

Even in the chill night air, Boyd's bald scalp glistened with perspiration. Fortunately for all of us, he let Torres do the talking.

"Mrs. Kimball, can you tell us what happened?"

"I don't know where to start," I began.

"Start with when we saw you last, outside the restaurant."

I told them about walking along the shadowy sidewalk, lost in my thoughts, and the sudden splat in front of me.

"She didn't make a sound on the way down."

My breath caught in my throat. They nodded grimly, and I managed to carry on.

"I thought maybe there was a party, people throwing things. But I didn't see any open windows or any people up there."

"Could you see the roofline?" Boyd asked.

We turned and looked up at the looming backside of the Hotel Kokopelli, now swept with spots of light from flashing police cars.

"I don't remember specifically looking all the way up there," I said, "but nothing grabbed my attention. I didn't notice anything untoward."

They said nothing.

I added lamely, "It was dark."

Torres and Boyd huddled in another muttered conference. I wondered if the senior officer was feeding Torres more instructions, or rating his interrogation of me. Must be tough, having that mean little pug shadowing you all day.

That reminded me of the Poodles, and I turned all the way around, shielding my eyes from the lights, surveying the crowd. I couldn't see Mitzi and Nannette anywhere.

Torres returned and asked me when I'd last seen Hilda alive. A shiver ran over me. Last time I saw Hilda, she was on her way to see Mr. Girard. Did I dare tell that to the police?

"Mrs. Kimball? Are you all right?"

"Yes, sorry. What?"

"When did you last see Miss Schmidt?"

"Before dinner," I said vaguely. "In the hotel."

"In her room?"

"Not exactly. In the penthouse hallway. I was on the elevator."

"She was going to her room?"

"I didn't actually see her go into a particular room before the elevator doors closed."

I didn't want to lie to the police, but I just could not bring myself to say something that might implicate Mr. Girard. Fortunately, Torres didn't wait for an answer.

"Was that officer still stationed in the corridor?"

I nodded.

"Okay, he'll know which room she went into. What time was this?"

"I don't know," I said. "I'm not sure. What time is it now?"

He looked me over. "Are you sure you're okay?"

"No, I'm not 'okay'. A good friend of mine just died here."

He mumbled something about giving me a moment, then chased after Boyd, who was yelling at someone down the way.

A white-uniformed paramedic appeared next to me. He barely came up to my shoulder, and he had a cowlick and freckles.

"Detective Torres asked me to look you over," he said. "You've had quite a shock."

"Yes, I have."

Opie shined a penlight into my eyes, one to the other, then back again.

"How do you feel now?"

"A little drained."

"That's natural. Are you injured anywhere?"

"No, I'm fine." Now that he mentioned it, my kneecaps hurt from contact with the sidewalk. Probably some bruising there, but the last thing I wanted was this little boy rolling up my pants to check 'em out, right in front of everyone.

"You're sure?"

"Please stop shining that light in my eyes."

"Sorry. They look fine. No concussion or anything."

"Young man. *I'm* not the one who fell on her head. I'm upset, not concussed."

"Yes, ma'am."

He scooted over to Torres and whispered something. They both looked at me like I was a crazy woman. It made me want to burst into tears again, but I sucked up a deep breath and called to the detectives, "Can I go now?"

Torres looked to Boyd, who rolled his eyes in answer. Everything the younger detective did exasperated him. Maybe he felt that way toward everyone he met. He'd certainly seemed exasperated by me. Jackass.

"Yes, ma'am," Torres said. "But we'll have more questions. You're going up to your room?"

I nodded, and he gave the okay. One last look at Hilda's body heaped under that sheet, and a lump rose in my throat. I ignored the shouts of reporters as I shoved through the crowd. Lights blinded me, but my jaw was clenched in determination and people got the hell out of my way.

Chapter 28

By the time the detectives knocked on my door an hour later, I felt much better. I'd said prayers for Hilda and taken time to count my own blessings. So important in a time of grief.

My recovery was fortified by two double margaritas delivered by room service (*thirty* dollars with tip, do not tell Harley). I don't approve of the abuse of strong drink and frankly don't like the taste of most liquor, but I find that two shots of tequila mixed into a colorful cocktail can be very therapeutic.

Torres and Boyd looked weary and cranky as they followed me to my armchair in the corner. I briefly wished I had margaritas to share with them, then realized that would be inappropriate because they were "on duty." I, however, was most certainly not on duty. A little loopy, to tell the truth.

"You better now?" Boyd cocked an eyebrow at the empty margarita glasses on the tray at my elbow. "Up to answering our questions?"

"I'm thine, fank you. Ahem. It has been a terrible shock. Hilda was so young. . . "

I let my voice trail off, as you do when discussing the recently deceased.

Boyd sighed and pulled a chair out from the desk in the corner. He wheeled it around to face me, then squatted on it like a fat toad. Torres leaned against the wall nearby.

"Just a few questions," Boyd said, "and then we can all go to bed."

Took me a second to understand that he meant we'd all go to our *respective* beds, but then the tequila might've made me slow-witted. Before I could get too confused, Torres butted in.

"You were one of the last people to talk to Miss Schmidt before she died."

"We only talked briefly. She was upset. She'd hidden something from her employer, and she felt bad about it."

"Yeah?" Boyd said. "What had she done?"

"Nothing, really. Met with some people who wanted Mr. Girard to star in a Western here in New Mexico. She'd gone to a party with them after the gala, and hadn't told him about it. A sin of omission, but she was afraid Mr. Girard would see it as a conspiracy."

Boyd nodded the whole time I spoke, as if he couldn't wait to jump in with another question.

"So she was upset."

"She seemed to feel better after we talked."

"She decided to tell Girard about going around behind his back?"

"I wouldn't put it that way, exactly, but yes, she went upstairs to talk to him. I rode up in the elevator with her, but I didn't actually see her go into his suite."

Still trying to cover for Mr. Girard. I couldn't seem to help myself.

"We talked to the officer up there," Torres said. "He saw her come out of Girard's suite forty-five minutes later. Said she looked like she'd been crying, but not so upset that she'd throw herself off the roof."

"She must've fallen or something," I said. "Did you say she was on the *roof*?"

"Fresh scuff marks on the parapet up there, right above where she landed."

"Whatever would she have been doing on the roof?"

"Smoking a joint," Boyd said. "Hotel employees go up on the roof to smoke, so there are cigarette butts all over up there. But we found a fresh roach near the scuffs."

"That doesn't seem like Hilda at all," I said. "Do you think she got stoned and fell off?"

"Maybe." Boyd seemed to chew that over, not liking the taste. "She was upset with her boss. Maybe she got stoned and jumped."

"That doesn't make a lick of sense," I said. "Hilda wasn't the least bit suicidal--"

"*Or*," he interrupted, "maybe somebody was up there with her."

"But who?"

"That's what we need to find out," Torres said. "Any ideas?"

"I haven't got a clue."

They were not amused.

"Let's start over," Boyd said. "Tell us the whole thing again."

FAN FAIR: THE OFFICIAL WEBSITE OF THE
INTERNATIONAL MICHAEL GIRARD FAN CLUB

11:14 p.m. March 25

From the President:

It is my sad duty to report the tragic loss of Mr. Girard's personal assistant, Hilda Schmidt. I bring you this terrible news from the Hotel Kokopelli in Santa Fe, where she fell to her death earlier this evening.

I talked with Hilda shortly before she died and, while she definitely was under some strain, she did not seem suicidal. I hope the police do not waste a lot of time on that line of inquiry.

However she died, it's a tragedy for the membership of the IMGFC, as well as for her family and friends. During Hilda's tenure with Mr. Girard, the relationship between him and the fan club has been wonderful. She was a hard-working young woman, and did her best to make things run smoothly.

Of course, she'd never before faced anything like the media circus that erupted here at the Santa Fe Silver Screen Society Film Festival after a young woman's body was found this morning in Mr. Girard's suite (we don't need to go into that again right now, and there's nothing new to report anyway, as far as I know).

I have not seen Mr. Girard since Hilda's abrupt demise, but I'm sure he is devastated by the loss.

One of her last acts on this Earth was to reschedule my face-to-face interview with Mr. Girard for ten o'clock tomorrow morning. I intend to keep that appointment, unless the police prevent me from seeing him. I will, of course, give you a full report.

Sorrowfully,
Loretta Kimball, president, IMGFC

Chapter 29

Fortunately, I found a sleeping pill in the bottom of my purse, or I never would've calmed enough to slumber. (I think it was a sleeping pill. Might've been a Tic-Tac for all I know, but it did the job. The tequila undoubtedly helped, too.)

I was sleeping soundly when my phone started playing "Happy Days Are Here Again" on the bedside table. Like most mothers, my first panicky thought when awakened by a phone is that something has happened to the kids. The phone's readout showed that it was 6:40 a.m., and the call was coming from my own home in Pandora.

"Harley?"

I sat up, head pounding, and looked around the dim hotel room. The night before came flooding back. Poor Hilda's deadly plunge. My sessions with the police. Bawling myself to sleep. No wonder my eyes felt like they were full of kaleidoscope gravel.

The phone kept playing its song, so I answered it. Harley didn't let me get past "hello."

"Good God, Loretta, I just saw the news about Hilda. Why am I always the last to know when you're up to your neck in trouble? Your friend dies in a mysterious fall, and do you turn to your husband in your time of distress? No, you do not. You don't even call him."

"Harley."

"I'm not done yet, Loretta. I should never have left you there in Santa Fe. I *knew* you would find a way to get into some kind of a situation. I never dreamed it might involve another dead girl, but I guess they party hard up there in The City Different."

"I haven't been to any parties, Harley."

"No, you've been too busy running from crime scene to crime scene."

"That's about enough now, Harley. You woke me up. I haven't had my coffee."

"Well, me neither. I'd just taken my first big mouthful when I saw the news on TV, and I spewed coffee all over the kitchen."

He was puffing, the way he does when he's really upset, so I tried to placate him (at least until I could get some caffeine into my system).

"Sorry, Harley. I should've called. But by the time the police were done with me, it was very late and I thought you'd be asleep."

"You could've woke me up for this one, Loretta."

"But you've been working so hard. You need your rest. What are you doing up so early anyway?"

He sighed at my obvious attempt to divert him, and told me the shed repairs were nearly complete and the storm had passed without drowning his plywood and stuff. I wasn't really listening. He clearly had the situation in hand, as I always trusted he would, and I was too busy firing up the little coffeemaker to follow the details.

"Anyway," he said, wrapping up, "I can probably get free by mid-morning to come get you."

"What?"

"I'll come get you. Just sit right there in your hotel room, and keep the door locked. I'll call you when I get to Santa Fe."

"Oh, there's no need to hurry up here, Harley. I'm perfectly safe. And I can't really go home yet anyway."

"Why not? The only reason you were staying up there was to help Hilda. She's beyond help now."

"The police told me to stick around. They may want to interview me again this morning."

"Why are they so interested in *you*?"

"Well, I am an eyewitness, Harley. I mean, the girl died right at my feet, practically, and--"

"*What*?"

I decided it would be better to start at the beginning. I told him about Hilda going off to see Mr. Girard and me going to dinner by myself, and how we'd met again on the sidewalk behind the Hotel Kokopelli. Harley was so quiet during the telling, I could hear his nose whistling.

"Well, I was in shock, of course," I said. "Mitzi showed up, and I blubbered all over her."

"You must've been in shock, if you got that close to Mitzi."

"Exactly. Those two detectives were all up in my face, too. Especially that horrid one, Boyd. Ooh, I'd like to pop him one."

"Now, Loretta--"

"You should've heard them, Harley, when they came up to my room. Badgering me. There's no other way to put it. They absolutely badgered me."

"I'm sure they had a lot of questions--"

"I told them everything I knew. I've got nothing to hide. I may be the *only* one in this hotel who's not harboring some dark secret."

"Getting a little dramatic there, hon."

"I can't help it. Those detectives annoy me so much. They're so used to talking to criminals, they've forgotten how to behave in polite company."

Harley sighed. "I'm sure you reminded them."

"They kept making me repeat my story, as if they could catch me in a lie. They're wasting their time interviewing *me*, a homemaker from Pandora, New Mexico, while someone is running around this town killing young women."

I had to pause for breath, and he saw an opportunity: "That's why I want you to come home right now."

"I can't, Harley. I still have things to do here. I've got to get ready for my interview with Mr. Girard."

Harley sputtered into the phone, and I pictured another coffee-spattered countertop. I swear, the man should carry paper towels on his person at all times.

"My appointment is for ten o'clock," I said. "And this time, that interview will take place. Nobody will stand in my way."

"I thought there's a cop outside his door."

"Yes, there is, and thank goodness for that, because otherwise they'd be trying to pin Hilda's death on Mr. Girard, too."

"How do you mean?"

"That officer saw Hilda go into Mr. Girard's suite, but he also saw her come back out later. He told the detectives she looked as if she'd been crying, but she was very much alive."

"So where did she go next?"

"Nobody knows. She got on the elevator, and wasn't seen again until she landed on the sidewalk."

"Somebody saw her."

"Maybe she wanted to be by herself. There are two or three stairways up to the roof, or so I'm told. Maybe she went up there to have a good cry."

"And then what? She fell?"

"Possibly. The detectives say they found marijuana up there, but that doesn't sound like Hilda, does it? Could've been left there by anybody, one of those bellhops--"

"You don't think she killed herself."

"No. Even if Mr. Girard had fired her or something terrible like that, she wouldn't have committed suicide. That girl had too much hope inside her."

"It's hard to tell sometimes, hon. People get depressed."

I knew Harley was thinking of his brother, Cliff, who died by his own hand twenty years ago. Poor troubled man. A little bit of Harley died that day, too.

"She fell," I said. "Or somebody pushed her."

"There you go. That's what I'm afraid of. You've got a killer on the loose up there, Loretta. I don't want you to be next."

"Nothing's going to happen to me, Harley. I'll stay in my room until it's time for my meeting with Mr. Girard. Then I'll come right back here and write up the interview for the website. By the time I get that posted and all, I'm sure we'll know more about what happened to Hilda. Then maybe the police will let me go home."

"They really told you to stay in Santa Fe?"

"I wouldn't make that up, Harley. They said I'm the primary witness. Apparently, that means they've got to ask me the same stupid questions every few hours."

"Don't get your blood pressure up, Loretta."

"I can't help it. Those poor girls! What if somebody did kill them both? These idiot detectives will never figure it out, and the killer will get away scot-free."

"Let the police do their jobs, Loretta. You just keep yourself safe."

"Of course I will, sweetie. Don't worry about me. You know what a careful person I am."

Harley sighed.

Chapter 30

Despite my assurances to Harley, I couldn't sit in my hotel room for hours, waiting for my interview with Mr. Girard. I was already a bundle of nerves.

Within an hour of my husband's call, I'd showered, dressed (jeans, low heels, lightweight purple sweater), done my face and hair, and downed all the coffee available in my room. My stomach was growling. I could've called room service and requested the Harley Special, but I wanted to get out and about. I had snooping to do.

The elevator was empty, and only a few sleepy newsmen were scattered around in the lobby. None seemed to recognize me from the night before.

Just as I thought I'd reach the coffee shop unscathed, Mitzi Tyner's unmistakable "yoo-hoo" froze me in place. The last thing in the world I needed right now.

"Lo-retta!"

I wheeled to shush her, but was too taken aback by her appearance. Mitzi wore jeans with a bright blue T-shirt tucked into her belt. Emblazoned across her (surgically enhanced) chest, in bright red, were the words: "Tyner Chevrolet, Pandora, NM."

Jewelry jingling, Mitzi clacked across the lobby toward me, shadowed by Nannette Hoch. Nannette was dressed the same as Mitzi, except she wore the tail of her loose T-shirt untucked, in keeping with her usual feed-sack fashion sense.

"What do you think?" Mitzi asked, pointing at her shirt, as if there could be any mistaking what she meant. "I figured that, with all these TV cameras around, we might as well get some free advertising."

I got a twitch in my left eye.

"We made up a shirt for you, too."

Nannette started digging in a shopping bag stuffed full of tourist detritus.

"No, thank you," I said. "I'm already dressed for the day."

"Come on, Loretta!" Mitzi said. "I'll bet you get interviewed all day today. It would tickle Long John if we all--"

"I'm trying to keep a low profile," I said tightly. "I most certainly do not want to be interviewed on television."

"But you saw what happened to that girl! Everybody will want to talk to you!"

I shushed her some more, but as usual, she was oblivious to everything except the next thought that might fall out of her own mouth.

"Why, I'd be surprised if you don't end up on the evening news!"

A couple of the dozing *paparazzi* stirred at the commotion, looking over at us, checking for famous faces.

I stepped closer to Mitzi and muttered, "If you don't keep your voice down, we'll both be on the news."

"We will?"

"Because I will kill you with my bare hands right here in this lobby."

Mitzi laughed gaily. "Oh, Loretta! You *slay* me!"

"Exactly."

Nannette growled protectively, but I ignored her.

"I've got a big day today," I said to Mitzi. "I don't have time to be chased around by the press."

"You might not have any choice," she said. "Everybody saw you last night."

"Would you *hush*? I don't want the attention. I need a quiet breakfast -- *alone* -- and time to get my thoughts together. You two are not helping."

"Thoughts about what?" Mitzi asked. "About what you're going to tell the police?"

"What? No. I've already talked to those detectives for hours. Surely they're done with me."

Nannette said, "I wouldn't be so certain."

I wondered what she was getting at, but it's hard to read Nannette. She always looks like she just found half a worm in her apple.

"The detectives are already back here this morning," Mitzi explained. "We saw them go upstairs. I'll bet they want to interview everyone again."

Great. No doubt they were headed to the penthouse, where I was bound to run into them again. But I didn't dare mention that destination to the Poodles.

"I, for one, am ready to tell everything I know." Mitzi proudly thrust forward her advertising. "I can't wait for Long John to see us on TV!"

More of the photographers eased off their seats and moved toward us. Made me think of crocodiles slithering off a riverbank.

"You're about to get your wish," I said to Mitzi. "Here they come."

She and Nannette turned toward the approaching cameramen, lining up to show off their T-shirts, and I used the distraction to slip away. I fled past the coffee shop and turned at the first corner I came to, which took me into a carpeted corridor. I glanced over my shoulder, but I seemed to have shaken the Poodles.

Sunshine gleamed through a glass door at the far end of the hall. I hurried toward the light.

Chapter 31

I was ill-prepared for the outdoors. First of all, I wore no coat, and the air was still crisp at nine o'clock in the morning. Secondly, my sunglasses were upstairs, and the bright sunshine made me squint like Mister Magoo.

The door opened onto a side street, and it was no wonder I hadn't noticed it before, as it was tucked between two fat evergreen shrubs. I took a deep breath of the cedar-scented air, and was rewarded with a whiff of tobacco smoke. Ick.

I stepped out of the shrubberies to find that same little bellhop who seemed to pop up everywhere. He gave me a smile, and cupped his cigarette out of sight.

"Don't mind me," I said. "I'll just stand upwind."

We did a little dance on the empty sidewalk to get situated, and it resulted in me facing away from the sun, so maybe I wouldn't go blind after all. He didn't seem to mind squinting. He was dressed in his uniform -- black slacks and short jacket -- and his polished shoes gleamed. His brass nametag said, "Jorge."

"I see you around here at all hours," I said. "Don't you ever get any time off?"

He raked a hand through his shiny black hair.

"I'm usually off on Saturdays, but no way I'd miss this film festival. I'm making a fortune off tips."

"Really? Lots of extra bags?"

"The hotel's full. Plus, all the TV guys in the lobby, waving twenty-dollar bills like Monopoly money. It adds up."

"I'm sure."

"I'm trying to buy a new car. One of those retro Mustangs, like the one Steve McQueen drove in 'Bullitt?'"

"Young man. Do I look like a connoisseur of automobiles to you?"

Jorge chuckled affably. His crooked smile reminded me of my son Ben, who always tried to grin his way out of trouble when he was a boy.

"Let's just say it's an expensive car," Jorge said. "A guy who wants one has got to do everything he can to earn extra cash."

I nodded understandingly, still thinking of Ben, who'd worked summers at KIMBALLS to earn enough to buy his first car. Counting out nuts and bolts all summer while his friends hung out at the swimming hole.

"You, uh, with one of the newspapers?" he asked. *That* snapped me back to the present.

"I most certainly am not. My name's Loretta Kimball. I'm president of the International Michael Girard Fan Club."

"Really?"

"Really."

"Cool."

I tried not to roll my eyes. Nothing delights me more than having some youngster pronounce me "cool."

He got a sly look on his dark face, and glanced up and down the street. "So you probably would be interested in what people are saying about Girard."

"What people?"

"Staff here in the hotel. Biggest bunch of gossips you've ever seen."

"And the hotel's full of people willing to pay for gossip. You're all getting rich spreading rumors."

He shrugged his narrow shoulders. "Saving up for that car."

"And you expect me to pay you, too?"

He took a last drag on the cigarette and pitched it into the street.

"Up to you. It's a juicy little nugget. You'll probably hear it for yourself soon enough."

"Wait a minute--"

"I've got to get back to work, ma'am. I'm on the clock here."

I could see where this was going. I snapped my purse open and reached inside.

"I will give you twenty dollars for this information you supposedly have. Not one penny more."

He looked around again, then took my twenty and made it vanish into his pocket. He leaned closer and said, "Your boy

Girard wasn't alone in that suite like he told the cops."

"What? When? Last night?"

"No, not last night. Nobody seems to know anything about that girl who fell. I'm talking about when that other girl died in Girard's room."

"They have no proof that she actually *died* there--"

"Girard ordered wine and cheese from room service a little before midnight. He tried to sign for it at the door, but the room service waiter had to go inside to set the tray down. The waiter definitely got a glimpse of someone else in that suite. In the bedroom."

My heart leaped. "Maria Mondragon?"

"He doesn't think so, but it was just a glimpse. But here's the clincher: There was a nightgown lying across the foot of the bed. He got a very good look at that. Unless Girard is a cross-dresser, there was a woman in that room with him."

I was surprised, of course, but I tried not to let on. Nobody had said anything about Mr. Girard having a woman in his room that night. A *nightgown*? Good heavens.

"Has anyone told the police?"

Jorge shook his head. "Hotel policy is 'keep your mouth shut.' The waiter's afraid of getting fired."

"You have no such fears?"

He grinned. "You should see that car."

Chapter 32

I didn't want to brave the lobby again, but I couldn't stay out on the sidewalk and freeze to death, either. I waited a minute after Jorge disappeared into the building, then went back inside.

The empty corridor was lined with unlabeled doors that probably led into service areas and stairwells, but I didn't try any of them. I would not climb four flights of stairs just to avoid the Poodles and the press. Not in these shoes.

I tiptoed to the mouth of the corridor, and peeked around the corner. I could see past the busy coffee shop (no Mitzi in there) to the lobby, where a pack of journalists generated the usual hubbub. They had someone cornered by the Kokopelli fountain, which meant their backs were to me. Perhaps I could slip past.

I still hadn't eaten, but it was too late now. My interview with Mr. Girard was coming right up, and I needed to return to my room for my tape recorder and notebook. And it might take a while to talk my way past the officer posted outside Mr. Girard's suite. I wasn't looking forward to that encounter. I was awfully tired of people telling me "no."

I kept a hand to my forehead as I skirted the press, hiding my face, but I needn't bothered. All attention was on the victim of their feeding frenzy.

Andre de Carlo stepped up onto the stone edge of the fountain pool so he suddenly was head and shoulders above the pack. Through a gap between cameramen, I could see Tony Lodge next to him. Both were dressed completely in black, as if they were Johnny Cash impersonators. Tony had his arms wrapped tightly around Andre's knees to steady him on his perch. This put his face and Andre's crotch in a perilous proximity, but neither of them seemed to mind.

"People!" Andre shouted. "People! Quiet!"

He clapped his hands scoldingly, as if chasing chickens, and the reporters finally settled enough to hear him. I paused at the fringe of the crowd. Close enough to hear, but with a clear line of escape to the elevators.

"Quiet, people!" This last one seemed gratuitous, as we'd all gotten pretty quiet already.

"I have a very brief statement," Andre said somberly. "I will not be taking questions."

Grumble, grumble from the press, but Andre talked over them.

"The Santa Fe Silver Screen Society lost a dear friend last night when Hilda Schmidt passed away here at the hotel."

"'Passed away?'" a deep voice boomed. "Didn't she throw herself off the roof?"

Andre glared in that direction. "The circumstances of Ms. Schmidt's demise are unknown. At least that's my understanding. Perhaps you have new information to share with the group?"

That got a laugh from the reporters. I didn't see anything funny about Hilda's "demise," and it pained me to remain silent.

"As I was saying," Andre shouted, "before I was so *rudely* interrupted--"

Another hoot from the press corps. Heathens.

"--Ms. Schmidt was a valued friend of our new film festival, this *infant* of ours."

Andre ran a hand over his partner's egg-shaped head, as if testing it for cracks. Tony clucked warmly at the attention.

"The police are investigating, of course," Andre said. "But they've assured us that her death has nothing, I repeat, *nothing,* to do with the film festival."

"Come on," a female voice shouted from the other side of the pack. "Two women dead at the same film festival?"

"Purely a coincidence," Andre said.

Tony, speaking directly into Andre's crotch, added, "As far as we know."

"As far as we know," Andre agreed.

"At this point in time." We could barely hear Tony's muffled addendum.

"At this point in time," Andre repeated.

He teetered for a second, and Tony hugged him tighter to steady him. Andre gripped Tony's head with both hands. The greedy cameramen moved in even closer, and I had a feeling this face-smashed-to-groin footage would get a lot of views on the Internet. For years to come.

Andre regained his balance, and Tony leaned back a little so he'd have room to breathe.

"Anyway, the police have encouraged us to continue all film festival activities as scheduled."

That drew a gabble of questions, but Andre ignored them.

"Our honored guest, Michael Girard, is scheduled to make appearances today, but we're not sure whether he'll be able to attend. He is, of course, quite upset over the unfortunate death of his personal assistant."

"Cops still have him on ice?"

"I don't know what you could possibly mean," Andre said. "Mr. Girard continues to be our guest here at the Hotel Kokopelli, and we've met regularly with him throughout this ordeal."

Andre's voice got a little tight toward the end; I felt sure he was lying. I had the feeling that no one other than Hilda and the police had met with Mr. Girard since this whole crazy mess began. Which made my interview with him even more special.

Chapter 33

By the time I arrived at the penthouse floor, my heart was absolutely pounding. The zigzag pattern of the carpet swam before my eyes. At the far end of the corridor, a hundred miles away, a black-uniformed officer stood at guard duty.

The doors nearly closed on me before I could work up the nerve to step off that elevator. Here I was -- finally -- at my Big Moment, my personal interview with my celebrity idol, and all I could think about was death.

I kept hearing Harley's words in my head. A killer loose in the hotel. A killer of women.

The deaths weren't coincidences and they weren't accidents. Andre de Carlo could spread that manure elsewhere. Someone *pushed* Hilda off that roof, and it was the same someone who deposited Maria in Mr. Girard's suite, dead or alive. Nothing else made sense. Two young women. Murdered. And what did they have in common? Their interest in Michael Girard.

Dare I ask him about the deaths? How could I not? Common courtesy required me to express my condolences for his loss of Hilda, so that brings up the topic right there. And once we're on the subject of dead women, how about that Maria Mondragon? And then there's the woman glimpsed in his suite the night Maria died. What was that about? Such burning questions made my planned interview seem like bland chitchat.

There was nothing in Mr. Girard's history (and, believe me, I would know) to suggest he could kill someone or drive someone to suicide or cover up a murder. But if he did indeed have a woman in his room that night, then at minimum he'd lied to the police. Which meant he was covering up something.

I was so caught up in my thoughts, I was face-to-face with the crew-cut cop before I was ready. He was a beefy young man with a straight line of a mouth. Looked as if he'd smiled once as a child and decided he didn't like it. His nametag said Mack.

"Ma'am."

I stammered through my name and affiliation and that I had a ten o'clock appointment with Mr. Girard. I left out the part about the appointment having been made by a woman who was currently deceased.

"Yes, ma'am. You're expected."

"I am? I mean, of course I am. I just expected more of a fuss. Everything else this morning has been much ado about nothing."

"Yes, ma'am," he said patiently. "I will need to look through your bag."

"My bag?"

"Strict security. For everyone's safety."

"Oh." I handed him my oversized purse. My mind whirred with what he might find in there -- loose tampons, unidentifiable pharmaceuticals -- but he gave the contents only a cursory glance. I realized he was checking for weapons.

"Good thing I wasn't packing."

I laughed. He didn't.

Instead, he handed me my bag and turned to knock on the door. Two sharp raps, a pause, then once more. A code. Gave me a little thrill.

A much bigger thrill was on the way. After a few seconds, we could hear the lock turn from inside. Officer Mack stepped out of the way as the door swung open.

I looked directly into the piercing blue eyes of Michael Girard.

Chapter 34

I felt breathless and dizzy and lightheaded and overheated. I finally knew what my Southern-bred mother meant when she spoke of suffering "the vapors."

My face was ablaze. Could this be a hot flash? The long-dreaded onset of menopause? Wouldn't that be the worst timing in the history of the world?

I tried to put that thought right out of my mind. No reason for me to go into some sort of metabolic collapse. It's not like I'd never met Michael Girard before. He's a man like any other, takes his pants off one leg at a time, and there was no reason we couldn't carry on a perfectly civilized conversation.

Then he flashed that familiar smile, and I melted all over again.

"Loretta," he said. "So nice to see you. Please come in."

I don't know how I managed to walk into that sunny suite. I was a puddle of protoplasm. A happy, sappy blob. A boneless chicken. But somehow I put one foot in front of the other and maneuvered through the doorway, passing within inches of my lifelong fascination.

When he gently closed the door behind me, my breath caught in my throat. For the first time ever, I was alone with Michael Girard. I turned toward him, my skin on fire, every nerve ending tingling like mad. How many times had I dreamed of this moment? How could it possibly live up to my fantasies?

I lifted my chin and looked right at him. Bold as you please. I didn't swoon or tear off my clothes or fall off my shoes. I took a deep breath, and let reality settle over me.

Michael Girard's famous blue eyes were hammocked by dark circles. The lines on his forehead seemed deeper, and his silvery hair seemed whiter, as if he'd aged years in the past few days. He was dressed in khakis and a linen shirt and the same grandfatherly slippers that I'd seen at the other suite. They seemed to fit him now.

I reminded myself that Mr. Girard was twenty years older than me, and he'd celebrate his seventieth birthday later this year. Seventy is considered still young these days. Still active and virile. But up close like this, without makeup or professional lighting or flattering camera angles, Mr. Girard looked old and sad.

"Won't you have a seat?"

He gestured me into a green armchair under a tall window, then sat in its mate, angled toward me. We both crossed our legs, and our dangling feet were only inches apart. I tore my eyes away from the ragged corduroy slippers, and met his steady gaze.

"I'm a little nervous."

He twinkled with amusement. "Don't be. We'll just have a chat. You can use a tape recorder, if you wish."

I'd completely forgotten about my mini-recorder. Blushing, I dug it out of my bag, along with my notebook and a Bic pen that wasn't too chewed up. I turned the recorder on, and set it on the arm of my chair, pointed toward Mr. Girard.

"There," I said. "I think I'm ready."

I wished he'd stop smiling, so I could concentrate.

"I'm sorry your visit to New Mexico has gone so badly," I said. "Hilda and the police and the negative publicity and all. Just awful."

His face sagged, and his eyes misted over. "It has been a difficult time. Hilda and I were very close, as you know. I'll miss her terribly."

"Of course you will."

"Nothing against the Land of Enchantment," he said, "but I wish I'd never come to this film festival. I had a bad feeling about it from the start, to tell you the truth, but Ava persuaded me it would be fun."

"Ava Andrews." I wrote her name in my notebook, as if there were any chance of me forgetting.

"Ava has remained a dear friend over the years. When she told me her little brother was starting this festival, it seemed only natural for me to help. Lend my name to the thing, make a few appearances, and in exchange I'd get an expenses-paid Santa Fe vacation."

I nodded understandingly. Who could turn down a deal like that?

"If I'd known then what I know now, I would've stayed home."

"You can't turn back the clock," I said automatically. "Regret doesn't solve anything."

"That's true, Loretta. Thanks for the reminder."

I felt myself flush. Who was I to spout advice to this distinguished man? He's facing the possible ruin of his career, and I'm throwing him old saws.

"I'd always hoped that you'd do a film project here in New Mexico, but I guess the opportunity never presented itself?"

"I came close once or twice, but the right project never gelled. It takes so much to put together a film, all the financing and script rewrites and finicky stars."

He smiled at that last part.

"I'd like to see more of New Mexico. I've spent this entire trip cooped up in hotel rooms."

"You can't really appreciate our endless skies unless you're outdoors. Sometimes, in Pandora, where I live, the air is so clear, I can see right up to heaven."

God, I sounded like Mitzi Tyner. The two of us ought to work for the Chamber of Commerce. We could get matching T-shirts. I changed the subject before I got completely derailed.

"Why not a Western? I've always thought you'd make a great cowboy. I'm sure other fans would agree."

"That's very nice. But I think I'm too old for roping cows."

He chuckled merrily, and for a moment the lines in his face curved into the movie-idol features so familiar to us all.

"They have stuntmen to do all that stuff."

"Good point, Loretta. I'll have to give that further consideration."

That teasing twinkle again. I had to force myself to look away.

"Hilda, bless her heart, told me she'd been encouraging you to take a role in 'Thunder Canyon.'"

His face darkened. "I'm surprised she discussed that with you."

"Just casual conversation. She told me she'd read the script and liked it."

He nodded, but said nothing.

"I guess Maria Mondragon read it, too, and had the same reaction."

"Is that so?"

"That's what Hilda said."

"You and Hilda must've had quite the extensive conversation. I didn't realize you were so close."

"We talked on the phone a lot. And I tend to be something of a mother hen when it comes to these girls. Can't keep from pecking around in their lives."

"Hmm. I believe that's the way the sitting hen becomes Sunday dinner."

He smiled without showing any teeth, and it gave me a chill. Was he trying to tell me something?

"Something my dear mother used to say," he added, but it didn't take the frost off. "She grew up on a farm, you know. As did I."

Ah. He wanted to lead me into the standard biography about growing up in the Midwest and discovering his gift for acting and moving to Hollywood. A tale, frankly, we've all heard before. I didn't know how long this audience with Mr. Girard would last, but I didn't want to waste time covering old ground.

"That's one thing Hilda and Maria had in common," I said. "They both had an interest in you doing 'Thunder Canyon.'"

He shifted in his chair.

"I'm sure they had many things in common," he said. "They were both young women, both connected to the film industry. I'm sure they knew many of the same people."

I nodded right along until he paused for air.

"I meant the thing they had in common *here*, at this film festival. They both seemed to be angling toward the same goal."

Mr. Girard sighed.

"Can I tell you something in confidence? Something I don't want to see printed on the website or anywhere else, ever?"

I gulped. Nodded.

"All right." He put his feet together on the floor and leaned toward me over his knees. "Here's the reason I don't want to do that project or any other Western. Are you ready?"

I nodded eagerly.

"Horses."

I blinked twice, then said, "I beg your pardon?"

"I'm deathly afraid of horses. Always have been. Big, dumb animals with hooves that can break your bones. Unpredictable brutes."

"But you grew up on a farm!"

"We grew corn. We had tractors. Some of our neighbors had horses, but I wouldn't get near them."

"Oh, there's nothing to be afraid of! I've been around horses all my life. They're not the brightest animals, true, but by and large, they are companionable. You rarely run across one that'll deliberately try to hurt you."

"They're not going to get the chance with me," he said.

"But that doesn't make any sense!"

"It's a phobia, Loretta. It doesn't have to make sense."

"Surely you could put on a cowboy hat and *pretend*. That is, after all, what you do for a living."

"To be any good in a Western, you must ride a horse," he said. "You can always tell which actors are comfortable astride those animals. I'd be laughable."

"Okay, but why the big secret? Why not just say, 'I'm afraid of horses, and you can stop bugging me about Westerns.'"

"It doesn't seem *manly*, you know? Afraid of horses."

"Everybody's afraid of something. I'm terrified of spiders, and they're much smaller than horses."

"I'd rather not share my phobias with the world. People see them as weaknesses."

"Unenlightened people."

"Trust me, Loretta. The unenlightened have the rest of us outnumbered."

"So it would seem."

Our faces were only two feet apart, so I had no protection when he turned on that magnetic smile. I felt drawn toward him, and I could tell he felt it, too. We had a moment, an undeniable spark between us. Not a prolonged flirtation or anything untoward. Just a *moment*. A sweet, magical, breathless moment. Then it was gone.

He sat back and looked past me, out the window, and I had a second to catch my breath. Good heavens.

A cloud drifted over his features. I knew there was nothing but blue, blue sky out that window. His storm was on the inside. Had our passing attraction unsettled him? Or was it revealing his fear to me?

"I'll never mention it to anyone," I said. "The horse thing."

"Of course you won't. I trust you, Loretta. Otherwise, you wouldn't be here."

I nodded and thanked him again for his time.

"Arranging this interview," I added, "was one of the last acts Hilda performed on this Earth, and I'm glad we're able to make her wish come true."

He misted up again, and I silently cursed myself. I kept saying the wrong thing.

"I talked to her right before she saw you last night," I said. "Even rode up here with her on the elevator."

"She was quite upset when she arrived. What did you say to her?"

"She did most of the talking. She felt like she had a lot to get off her chest, if you'll pardon the expression."

"Yes, that's what she said to me."

I waited, but he added nothing further.

"She told me about that party," I said. "She felt bad about that."

Nothing.

"She was worried you would think she'd been going around behind your back."

He laughed, a quick, ugly bark with no merriment in it.

"Exactly what she *was* doing. *Selling* access to me. For drugs. It was disgusting!"

231

"Whoa. *Drugs*?"

"I suppose she failed to mention that part to you."

"She said she went to a party."

"Yes, where she was provided with booze and *drugs*. Marijuana, pills, I don't know what all. I don't approve of drugs, never have. They're everywhere in Hollywood, and I've been forced to look the other way my entire career. I told Hilda when I hired her, I've got a zero tolerance policy."

"People make mistakes at parties--"

He shook his head to stop me. "Don't you see? Because Hilda misbehaved, the filmmakers *had* something on her. They could use it as leverage to get access to me."

"They did that?"

"No. Not yet."

I frowned at him. "Then how can you say--"

"Well, it's all blown up *now*, hasn't it? They can't very well force an audience with me when there's a policeman stationed outside my door!"

He caught himself getting loud, and snapped his mouth shut. Stared out the window some more.

"I'm sorry," he said finally. "I'm under a lot of stress."

"You're grieving. Hilda's been by your side for years, and now she's gone. It must feel like part of you is missing."

He nodded somberly.

"She never let on to me about any drugs," I said gently. "And I don't think she would've let somebody blackmail her, either. She came here last night to tell you the whole truth, I'm sure of that."

Another nod.

"So she went to a party," I nudged. "They drank and did drugs and whatever. Is that all she confessed to you?"

He hesitated before he nodded again. Hmm.

"You didn't hear this party? Right down the hall?"

"I didn't hear anything," he said. "I take sleeping pills every night."

"And you were all alone?"

He frowned. "Why are you asking me these questions? I thought we were going to talk about movies. For the fans."

"I'd love to do that," I said, "but the fans watch the news, too. They need to hear from you about what happened that night and what happened to Hilda. Let's walk through it real quick, and get it out of the way."

"I don't think so, Loretta. Tell my fans that I'm in mourning for both young women. That's good enough."

"But don't you want to address the rumors? All the stuff that's been on the news?"

"I never dignify rumors with a response. It's just digging a dirty hole deeper."

"I understand that, but this is a forum for you. I mean, your attorneys will clear everything first--"

"No. That's off-limits. End of discussion."

I never appreciate it when someone unilaterally declares the end to a debate. It's not polite. It is, essentially, telling the other person (me, in this case) to shut the hell up.

"Well," I said. "You'd better brace yourself for the next round of rumors. The hotel staff has been talking to reporters. I heard about it when I was on my way here."

His frown was a vivid warning, but I couldn't seem to stop talking.

"They're saying you had a woman in your suite the night Maria died. A room service waiter saw someone in the bedroom."

A flush crawled up Mr. Girard's neck, past his sharp cheekbones, all the way to his hairline. Much like watching mercury rise in a thermometer.

"Who did this waiter supposedly see?"

"No one knows. He got just a glimpse."

Mr. Girard steepled his fingers in front of his chin. Trying for a serene pose, I suppose, but his hands were trembling.

"So he saw nothing," he said. "That's the way these things always go. Some wild allegation that's just vague enough that it can't be checked out. Everyone runs around cackling, and nobody cares what's true or false. I thought you were better than that, Loretta."

"I only told you about this rumor to warn you what's coming next. If there was no woman in your room, say so, and we'll move on."

He let the silence build a long time before he finally said, "I thought you were a loyal person."

"No one is more loyal than me, Mr. Girard. I'll stand by you until the bitter end. But your fans deserve to know--"

"This interview is over."

"Oh, there's no reason to--"

He snatched the mini-recorder off the arm of my chair.

"I'll keep this. I'll see it's returned to you after my attorneys make sure this conversation has been erased. If you repeat anything we've said, anywhere, you'll be hearing from those same attorneys."

I couldn't have been more stunned if he'd brained me with a hammer. I stammered through an apology and more assurances, but he coldly pointed toward the door.

"You can see yourself out."

Chapter 35

I don't know how long I stood frozen outside Mr. Girard's suite. I heard the door clunk shut behind me, but I couldn't move, immobilized by the horror I felt.

"Ma'am? Are you all right?"

The stone-faced officer swam into focus. I could tell he was concerned because a single furrow had formed between his eyebrows.

I was most certainly not "all right." I was *devastated.* The one person I adored most in the whole world (after Harley and my children) had told me to get lost. And called me a traitor. Common courtesy prevented me from unloading all that onto Officer Mack. I made some noises about being fine and wished him a good day or year or life or something. Then I blindly began the lonely trek of that long corridor.

My eyes burned, but I would not -- repeat would *not* -- burst into tears while that policeman was watching. I sucked air through my teeth, panting, the way they teach you to do during childbirth. This emotional pain was right up there with the physical pain of labor. With childbirth, you get a prize at the end. I had no such consolation now.

How had the interview gone so terribly wrong? Yes, I might've been a little pushy, a little nosy. But there was no reason for him to turn so icy and mean.

I'd remained devoted to Mr. Girard all these years partly because he'd always seemed such a gentleman, on-screen and off. I never imagined he could be so abrupt and harsh with another human being, especially one who's always had his best interests at heart. If he didn't want to answer my questions, he could've just said so. He didn't need to accuse me of being a gossip and a snoop.

By the time I arrived at the elevator, I'd worked myself up into an indignant snit that burned away any danger of tears. I punched the elevator button so hard that I broke a nail. This made me say a very bad word. I glanced back at Officer Mack, who'd resumed his stance before Mr. Girard's door, but he didn't seem to have heard.

A bell dinged and the doors slid open and I stepped inside the blessedly empty elevator. One floor down, then stomp-stomp to my own room. A man in a jogging suit emerged from a door down the way, but he got one look at me and went back into his room.

My cardkey didn't work on the first try, and I gave it another vicious swipe through the reader. I let the heavy door slam shut behind me.

Housekeeping had cleaned my room while I was gone. I threw my purse onto the freshly made bed and plunked down in the nearest chair and buried my face in my hands. I sat like that for a minute, expecting a good cry now that I was alone, but the tears wouldn't come.

"Screw it," I said aloud. "He's not worth bawling over."

The sound of my own voice helped me pull myself together, as it so often does. I stood and checked my face in the wall mirror. Not too bad. A little blotchy, but my eye makeup needed only the slightest touching up.

I would not let this horrible misunderstanding with Mr. Girard ruin my life. I would not even allow it to ruin my day. I'd give us both a little time to cool off, then I'd contact him, ask if we could start over. No idea how I'd make contact, now that Hilda was gone, but I'd find a way.

FAN FAIR: THE OFFICIAL WEBSITE OF THE
INTERNATIONAL MICHAEL GIRARD FAN CLUB
11:22 a.m. March 26

From the President:

It is my sad duty to report that my long-awaited interview with Mr. Girard, scheduled for today, was unavoidably interrupted. I am unable to report any of our conversation at this time, but hope to bring you details in the near future.

In the meantime, I remain at the Santa Fe Silver Screen Society Film Festival and will deliver updates as developments warrant.

Sincerely,

Loretta Kimball, president, IMGFC

Chapter 36

I'd no sooner closed my laptop than someone banged on the door. I gave myself a quick check in the mirror and went to the peephole. The fisheye lens showed the bleary, smeary mug of Detective Nelson Boyd. His partner, Rick Torres, bobbed behind him like an excited puppy.

Detective Boyd slapped the door with his meaty hand, right in front of my face, startling the petunias out of me. I snatched open the door and shouted, "Stop that! Don't you know it's rude to make so much noise in a hotel? What if people are still sleeping?"

Boyd was not cowed. People like him do not care about the needs of others. He pushed past me into my room, Torres right on his heels.

"Do come in," I said, dripping sarcasm. They acted like they didn't even hear.

"Come over here and sit down," Boyd said.

I still stood by the open door. It hadn't even crossed my mind to make a break for it until he started being Mr. Bossymouth.

"Come on. Sit down."

I was wearing the wrong shoes for sprinting, so I closed the door and crossed the room to the chair he indicated. He scooted the other chair up close. Torres sat on the foot of the bed, so they sort of had me cornered there in my own room. I did not care for it one bit.

"What do you want? I've already answered all your questions."

"We got new questions," Boyd said. "You went upstairs and talked to Girard."

That wasn't a question, so I didn't bother to deny it.

"Officer Mack said you seemed upset when you came out."

Still not a question, but I could see where he was headed.

"I was upset. Mr. Girard canceled my interview in midstream."

"How come?"

"I don't see how that's any business of yours."

"Lady," Boyd said, leaning closer, "it's *all* police business until I say otherwise."

I pressed myself back into my chair to get some distance from him. Hated to give any ground, but I didn't want to be hit by flying spittle.

"I liked it better," I said, "when your partner was asking the questions."

Torres smiled before he caught himself. Boyd continued as if I hadn't spoken.

"What did you say that got Girard bent out of shape?"

"Why in the world would you *assume* it was something *I* said?"

"I've talked to you before," Boyd said. "Every time, I come away wanting to kill myself."

"What a terrible thing to say."

Torres cleared his throat, but Boyd didn't get the signal, too busy glaring at me. Torres grasped his partner's shoulder and gently pulled him back.

"Let me," he said. "What my partner means to say is that your conversation with Mr. Girard could be very important to our investigation. You wouldn't want to get in the way of our investigation, would you?"

"Of course not. No one wants this resolved more than I do. But Mr. Girard threatened me with attorneys if I repeat anything--"

"Don't worry about that," Boyd said. "They come after you, they'll have to come through us."

I paused. If Torres had made the same pledge, I would've dismissed it immediately. Going through him would be like going through a bead curtain. But Boyd was such a nasty man that I believed he could ward off most anything, including a plague of lawyers.

"I asked Mr. Girard about Hilda and Maria," I said, "and whether their deaths had anything to do with him."

"Yeah? What did he say?"

"He got upset, as if I had accused him of something, when in fact I was simply trying to look out for his best interests--"

Boyd held up a hand to stop me.

"What did *he* say?"

"He said Hilda had confessed to him that she went to a party on the night Maria Mondragon was killed."

"A party."

"Yes, with some film people. I guess it got a little wild -- he said drugs were involved -- and he was very upset with her."

Unprompted, Torres asked, "Was Maria Mondragon at this party?"

"What? No. She was busy getting killed and deposited in Mr. Girard's suite."

Boyd's greasy eyebrows shot up. "Girard said that?"

"No! We hardly talked about Maria at all!"

"I thought you said you asked him about the deaths."

"I did. But we mostly talked about Hilda, not Maria. He and Hilda have worked together for years and--"

"But he was ready to can her over this party?"

"I never said that. He was upset because he felt like she was sort of selling access to him."

"By going to a *party*?"

"The timing was really bad. It looked like she was urging him to do this Western because she partied with the filmmakers. In fact, she told me herself that it was because the script for 'Thunder Canyon' is really good."

Boyd rolled his eyes.

"That's all we talked about before Mr. Girard got all huffy and ordered me out of his suite."

"Why did he do that?" Torres asked.

"He thought I was trying to stir up gossip, when I was trying to do exactly the opposite. But he wouldn't listen--"

"What did he say about Maria Mondragon?" Boyd asked.

"What? Nothing! I told you that."

"You said you 'hardly' talked about her at all. What did he say?"

"Just that she and Hilda had a lot in common, both being young women in the film industry. Probably knew a lot of the same people."

"That's it?"

"We really focused on Hilda and on making Westerns, not on--"

"Did he say anything about one woman killing the other?"

"*What*?"

"Several witnesses say Maria was flirting with Girard," Boyd said. "Maybe Hilda didn't like that. Maybe Hilda found her in Girard's suite."

"She had a key," Torres said.

"Maybe she found Maria in there and bashed her one."

"That is complete and utter nonsense," I said. "Hilda would not hurt a fly. She was too gentle for that, and too nervous besides."

"It's the high-strung ones who surprise you," Boyd said. "Maybe she snapped. Then she felt so bad about it that she killed herself."

"You can't seriously believe--"

"We need to talk to Girard again," Boyd said to his partner. "Find out what exactly Hilda Schmidt *confessed* to him before she threw herself off that roof."

"We already covered that with him," Torres said.

"We're about to do it again," he said. "Let's go."

They got to their feet.

"Hey," I said. "Are you even listening to me? I talked to Hilda more than once between the two deaths. There's no way she killed somebody. I would've been able to tell."

"Yeah, right," Boyd said. "You could read her so well because you two spent so much time together."

"We have spent hours on the phone over the past few years, but I suppose that's not good enough for you."

Boyd snorted. Torres gave me a silent shrug before he followed his partner to the door.

"That would be awfully tidy," I called after them. "Blame Maria's murder on Hilda, and both are sewn up nicely. No charges, no trial. Nobody famous gets in trouble."

They didn't even look back. The door slammed shut behind them.

Chapter 37

I simply wanted a quick bite to eat. Was that too much to ask? After all the upset and interrogation, I needed nourishment. I considered room service, but that might require a second mortgage. Besides, better that I be out and about, crossing paths and rubbing elbows. Maybe I'd hear something about the murders.

That's how I thought of the deaths now. "Murders." Those detectives might think Hilda killed herself, but I still felt in my bones that someone else was responsible. But who?

I didn't get a chance to sort through it further because I was assaulted as soon as the elevator doors opened in the lobby.

"Loretta!"

Mitzi and Nannette stood just outside the door in their promotional T-shirts. Waiting for an elevator, I suppose, when the door opened on mine. The timing was emblematic of my bad luck where Mitzi Tyner was concerned.

"We've been looking all over for you!"

No escape. I stepped off the elevator, right into their clutches. Mitzi grasped my elbow as if we were old friends rather than old rivals and steered me toward a corner of the lobby. Scrawny Nannette guarded our flank.

"Tell us about your interview with Mr. Girard."

I went to shush her, then realized there were no reporters or photographers within shouting distance.

"Where did everybody go?"

"Who?"

"The news crews."

"Oh, them. Once they saw we were getting into every shot to promote Tyner Chevrolet, they left."

"They left."

"Yeah." She frowned for just a second before again flashing her beauty-queen teeth. "But I'm pretty sure we got on 'Good Morning, America!'"

Nannette nodded vigorously, which looked for all the world like someone shaking out a dust mop.

Leave it to these two to find a way to scare off the American news media. Good thing, though, because Mitzi seemed incapable of lowering the volume.

"Come on, Loretta, what did he say?"

"I don't want to talk about--"

"Did he confess?"

"What? No! He doesn't have anything to confess. He didn't *do* anything."

Listen to me, defending Mr. Girard, even after the way he'd treated me. Knee-jerk reaction, based on years of loyalty.

Mitzi leaned in closer. "He *knows* things, though, doesn't he? That's why the police are keeping him locked up."

"He isn't locked up. There's a policeman outside his suite to protect him from the *paparazzi*. Little did we know we could've just stationed you two there in your T-shirts."

Mitzi laughed gaily, which made Nannette scowl all the harder. To her, laughter was the music of the devil.

"Did you even *talk* to him?" Nannette said. "Or was your interview mysteriously *canceled* again?"

Ooh, she could get under my skin.

"Yes, I talked to him, but it was a private conversation, and frankly none of your beeswax."

"Private?" Mitzi said. "I thought you were interviewing him for your website."

"Well, I was--"

"That's hardly private, now is it? I mean, you don't have a bazillion readers or anything, but still the Internet is a public--"

"Stop! Our interview didn't go well, okay? He's too upset about Hilda."

"So he cut it short, huh?"

"He had other commitments," I said. "It's a very busy time, and he's without a personal assistant now."

"Aw, that's too bad," Mitzi said, but I could tell she didn't mean it. "I know you were looking forward to that interview."

"Yes, but--"

"Your face-to-face meeting with the big star," Nannette said. "Lah-de-dah."

I resisted the urge to punch her pinched little mouth, but the effort exhausted me. I sighed deeply.

"Can I go now? Are you finished taunting me?"

"Taunting?" Mitzi made her painted eyes go wide. "That's not what were doing, Loretta. We were genuinely interested."

"Bull. You two were hoping it went badly, so you'd have another reason to feel superior and smug."

"You were the smug one," Nannette snapped. "Lording it over the rest of us, all the while up to your neck in *evil*."

Her face squinched up into such a tight scowl, it made me think of a bellybutton.

"What the hell are you talking about, Nannette?"

"Never mind." Mitzi grasped Nannette's narrow shoulders and turned her away. "We don't need to get into all of that right now."

"All of *what*? What is she talking about?"

"Nothing, nothing." Mitzi pushed Nannette along, and for once it was all I could do not to follow *them*.

"Is she accusing me of something?"

Mitzi looked over her shoulder at me and said archly, "We all have our suspects, don't we?"

I was so flabbergasted that they were almost out of earshot before I was able to respond.

"I suspect you two are *nuts*."

Chapter 38

I resisted the urge to chase after the Poodles. I could not concern myself with the paranoid fantasies of small-town gossips.

What I needed, and quick, was some food. Rather than go to the coffee shop and wait for them to clear the cobwebs off Today's Special, I got the heck out of the Hotel Kokopelli.

Still sunny outside, but with a stiff breeze that made me walk briskly. I went toward the plaza, weaving between waddling tourists on the shaded sidewalks. I passed a couple of crowded cafes, but thought I might expire if I had to wait for a table. I'd nearly resigned myself to something from a sidewalk vendor when I spotted a familiar face among the strolling shoppers. Kip Kaplin, looking furtive as ever.

I came up behind him and said, "Just the man I was looking for."

He turned and his eyes went wide behind his narrow glasses.

"I need to talk to you," I said. "Let me buy you lunch."

We were, as it happened, standing right in front of a restaurant called Mirabella. Kip had been dodging through tourists to reach the place, and he couldn't very well deny it now. The cafe had a suspicious number of empty tables.

Probably cost a fortune, but it would be worth it if I could get Kip to sit still for a minute.

"Come on," I said. "How often does someone offer you a free lunch?"

He snorted. "You're kidding, right? I work in Hollywood. I haven't bought my own lunch in years."

I made a show of looking all around. "I don't see anyone else offering at the moment."

I held the door open for him, and he seemed to weigh for a moment the idea of fleeing. Then he sighed and went inside and asked for a table for two.

A dark-eyed hostess led us to a table off by itself, which was perfect. I had some questions for Kip, but I didn't want anyone to overhear the answers. Mr. Girard's name was bound to come up.

Mirabella's menu was the size of a billboard, and Kip hid behind his. His knee bounced nervously, making the whole table jitter. He wore faded jeans and a shiny gray blazer over an open-collar shirt. A chunky wristwatch. I bet everyone he knew in Hollywood dressed exactly the same way.

A chirpy waitress appeared at our table. She wore dozens of bracelets and an unappetizing silver ring through her eyebrow. She recited the specials, but I wasn't listening. I was too busy trying to size up Kip.

When the waitress finally stopped chirping, I ordered a Cobb salad because you can always count on those. (I suspect all Cobb salads nationwide are manufactured in a central location.) Kip ordered a prime rib platter, pointing out it was the most expensive thing on the menu at forty-two dollars. I managed not to flinch, and he rewarded me with an oily smile.

My phone started blaring in my purse, and I dug it out and silenced it with my thumb. The call was from Harley's number, but this was no time for an update from home. I set the phone on "vibrate" and dropped it back into my bag.

"Sorry about that," I said. "Don't you hate people who talk on the phone in restaurants?"

He frowned. "I do that all the time."

"I'm sure you don't mean to." I smiled at him. "I'm so glad I spotted you outside because I wanted to ask you some questions about that party the other night."

"Um." His eyes darted around the restaurant, as if he were checking for exits. "What party would that be?"

"The party in your suite," I said. "The one Hilda attended."

"Not really a party. Just a few friends sitting around, winding down."

"That's what I call a party."

"Yeah, but it's not like there were invitations and all. It was impromptu."

"Ah. Often the way with late-night parties."

"Sure."

"Hilda told Mr. Girard you guys had drugs at that party. He got upset with her."

Kip's eyes widened.

"We had a few drinks, smoked a joint. No big deal. Why would he care about a quiet little party?"

"Guess he has a strict code of behavior for his personal assistants."

Kip laughed, as if the very idea of a moral code was hilarious. I didn't see anything funny about it, but before I could follow up, the waitress frisbeed a basket of bread onto the table between us.

"Your food will be right out," she chirped, in case we'd had any doubts, then jangled away.

Once she was out of earshot, I said, "Mr. Girard chewed Hilda a new one over that party. She was afraid she might be fired."

"That's crazy. What does he care what she did in her off hours?"

"She was pushing your movie on him. So it looked bad, see? A conflict of interest."

"Jesus," he said. "Is that all? Is that why she jumped off the roof?"

He'd gotten a little loud there at the end, but I kept my voice low.

"Hilda was sensitive, but she wasn't suicidal. I don't think she jumped."

"Yeah? Then what happened?"

"Somebody pushed her."

He ran his hands back and forth along the edge of the table. "Why would somebody do that?"

"You tell me."

"How would I know? I partied with the chick one time. I don't know her life story."

He looked toward the kitchen. Seemed to be weighing whether the prime rib platter was worth waiting for. I talked faster.

"How did she end up in your suite?"

"How do you think? Sean and I asked her over. Really, you're making too much of this. We had a few laughs. It was no different from any other night."

"Might've seemed like a bigger deal to Hilda. Might've made her feel that she owed you in some way."

"Owed me? For what?"

"She told Mr. Girard the 'Thunder Canyon' script is really good."

"It *is* really good. I wouldn't be pushing this project if I didn't believe in the script."

"When did you show it to her?"

"The script? That night. At the aforementioned party."

The oily smile again. I felt like smacking him.

"Look," he said, "I paid plenty for that suite, just for the opportunity to put that script into the right hands."

"I thought the VIP suites were comped by the organizers."

He gave me a pained look. "Yeah, right. But what's the secret to success? Proximity. That's what you pay for. You think it was just good luck that I was next door to the actor I was trying to recruit? How naive are you?"

That got my hackles up, but I tried not to let it show.

"Just so you could show that script to Hilda?"

Again with the look. "No. So we could show it to Michael Girard. Hilda was the gatekeeper. That's all."

"Then why did you show the script to Maria Mondragon?"

"What?"

"Hilda said Maria had seen the script, too, and really liked it. But she couldn't put it in Mr. Girard's hands, could she?"

Kip shook his head. "It wasn't like that. We were just passing it around, showing them the good parts."

"When? At that party?"

"What? No. I didn't mean we were literally passing it from hand to--"

"Was Maria Mondragon at that party?"

"No! Where would you get a crazy idea like that?"

"She was on the penthouse floor for some reason."

"Nothing to do with me."

"Is that what you told the police?"

"What I told the police is none of your business. In fact, I don't even know why I'm having this conversation."

"The prime rib platter."

"Yeah, well, I don't need a free lunch this bad."

He stood and tossed his napkin on the table.

"Oh, don't go away mad," I said. "Your food will be here any second."

Kip stomped out of the restaurant and disappeared from sight.

The waitress showed up a minute later, carrying two platters of food. She seemed perplexed by Kip's absence, but I told her not to worry about it and she set down the plates and jingled away.

The Cobb salad was straight from Central Casting, but the prime rib was surprisingly tasty.

Chapter 39

I waited until I got back to my room to check my phone messages. Seven voicemails, all from Harley.

Oops.

I could tell he was torqued when he answered the phone because he said, "Hold on," then not another word until he'd marched into his office. I could picture every step he took because 1) the store's so familiar after all these years and 2) we'd suffered through this routine before.

His door slammed.

"Now," he said, "you want to tell me where you've been the last few hours?"

"I just came from lunch. What's the matter with you?"

"I called and called, and you never answered. Last I heard, you were going off to your interview with Mr. Girard. Then not another goddamned word."

"Harley Kimball! There is no reason to take the Lord's name in vain."

"I'm sorry, but I didn't know what had happened to you, Loretta. For all I knew, the killer got you. I was worried sick."

"Oh, Harley, you let your imagination run away with you. I was perfectly safe the whole time."

"Then why didn't you answer your phone?"

I finally got it. I go to see Mr. Girard, my lifelong idol, in a *hotel room*, and then Harley can't reach me. For hours. That could look a little suspicious, especially to someone far away in Pandora. Harley always says he doesn't have a jealous bone in his body, but bones aren't where it's kept. Jealousy lives in the heart, right next to love.

"I was in a restaurant, Harley. You know I don't take calls in restaurants."

"For *hours*?"

"Before that I was in my room, posting to the website, which you can check for yourself. And before that I had a very brief interview with Mr. Girard."

"Brief?"

"It went poorly," I admitted. "We got crossways with each other, and he threw me out of his suite."

"What?"

"*And* he kept my tape recorder!"

"Why?"

I told him how I peppered Mr. Girard with questions, and how he didn't respond well. The purloined recorder. The threatened attorneys. Detectives Boyd and Torres and their loopy theory. Mitzi and Nannette and their T-shirts.

By the time I got through all that, Harley didn't seem to mind that I gave short shrift to lunch. I didn't mention Kip Kaplin's snitty little performance or the prime rib platter. Harley would see the MasterCard charge from Mirabella soon enough.

We could talk about it then.

"I set my phone to 'vibrate' while I was eating. Must've been a thrill for my purse."

Not even a chuckle.

"I'm coming to get you," he said. "I can be there in three hours."

"Don't be silly. I'm fine."

"You should be home."

"It's too late to check out of the hotel now," I said. "We'd have to pay for tonight anyway. Why don't you come get me in the morning when you're fresh?"

He grumbled, but I asked him about things at the store and that steered him away. The welders were done with the shed repairs. Harley's employees had fixed the forklift and were putting all the lumber back where it belonged.

"You're not letting Bill Hickenlooper anywhere near that forklift, are you?"

"No, no. Lesson learned there."

"Okay," I said. "You get out there and supervise those people. Tomorrow I'll come home."

He sighed. "Will you keep your phone turned on?"

"Yes, hon. I'm sorry."

"You don't have to apologize."

"I never meant to worry you."

"I'm fine," he said gruffly. "I'll see you in the morning."

"I'll be ready. And I'll be nice and careful between now and then."

"Okay then. Love you."

"I love you, too, Harley. Only you."

Chapter 40

I felt better after talking with Harley, but the conversation reminded me I was running out of time. In less than twenty-four hours, I'd be back home in Pandora.

Everyone else would leave soon, too. Film festival activities were scheduled to wrap up this evening. The stars would go home to Hollywood, and everyone would try to forget about the two dead girls, bless their hearts. Those idiot detectives would see that their deaths were swept under the rug. And somebody would get away with murder.

I couldn't stand it. I had to *do* something, but what? Pacing around my room, phone in hand, I thought back over what I'd learned so far. Did I have a single thing I could take to the police?

Maria Mondragon *might've* been at that party with Hilda and the "Thunder Canyon" boys, though Kip denied it. That would explain what Maria was doing on the penthouse floor, but it wouldn't explain how she ended up in Mr. Girard's suite.

Was Maria the woman glimpsed by the room service waiter? Was that her nightgown on the bed? Would she have brought a *nightgown* along for party-hopping? Or had it been a rendezvous? If it was even Maria at all. If it was someone else, why hadn't that woman come forward to provide Mr. Girard with an alibi?

Could it have been *Hilda* the waiter saw? She said she returned Mr. Girard to his room before she went to Kip's party. Had she spent more time with her boss than she'd let on? Time that involved a nightgown? Maybe that's why she was so broken up over Mr. Girard. Maybe their fight had been about more than business.

Hmm. I couldn't see it. Hilda was always talking on the phone about her loser boyfriends. Never a hint that she might have a crush on her boss. The age difference was too great, I suppose, though it was hard to see how any woman could withstand daily doses of Mr. Girard's charisma.

I wondered if Officer Mack was the one who saw Hilda leave Mr. Girard's suite. Maybe he knew more about what happened in that suite, and how she seemed when she emerged. Was there any chance he would tell me about it?

No time like the present. I checked myself in the mirror, patted my uncontrollable curls, and went upstairs.

The long hallway was empty except for Officer Mack, who stood at the far end, stony as an Easter Island egghead. I walked right up to him, but got only the barest glimmer of recognition.

"I'm feeling much better now," I said, smiling to beat the band. "Hope you weren't too alarmed earlier when Mr. Girard, um, asked me to leave."

He shrugged.

"Little misunderstanding," I said brightly. "Heard anything out of there since then?"

He shook his head.

"Pretty quiet otherwise, huh?"

He nodded.

"I was wondering about something. Were you the one on duty last night, when Hilda Schmidt came out of that room?"

He shook his head.

"Do you know who was?"

Another shake.

"You're quite the conversationalist, aren't you?"

"So I'm told."

We stood in silence for a while. I'd run out of questions, and he didn't seem to have anything to add. Nothing from inside Mr. Girard's suite. Nothing more to say.

I thanked him and turned away, toward the distant elevator. I would've loved to go up and down that hallway, banging on doors and demanding answers, but I couldn't very well do that with Officer Mack watching. Instead, I walked slowly, listening at doors, hoping to hear a clue drop.

A TV played loudly behind one door, but otherwise the penthouse floor was quiet. A door opened up ahead, near the elevator, and Ava Andrews stepped into the corridor.

She was dressed in jeans and sneakers and a baggy green sweater, but there was no mistaking her. She glanced toward me, then put on big black sunglasses. The standard celebrity disguise. Who do they think they're fooling?

I hurried to catch up to her.

Chapter 41

Ava Andrews looked less glamorous up close. Her forehead had a tight cosmetic sheen (there's a reason they call it *plastic* surgery), but the stringiness at her neck gave away her true age, which was close to Mr. Girard's.

She faced the elevator door, deliberately not looking at me as I puffed beside her.

"Miss Andrews? Hi. I thought that was you!"

She smiled without showing any teeth, then went back to staring at the elevator door. Probably afraid I'd ask for her autograph, which would've been a temptation under normal circumstances. But I had other things on my mind now.

"Pretty quiet here on the penthouse floor today."

She nodded, but still didn't look at me.

"Guess it's been loud all weekend, though. Big parties and stuff?"

"I wouldn't know. I'm not much of a party person."

"Early to bed for you, huh? How did you get any sleep with all the coming and going up here?"

"It wasn't so bad."

The elevator door dinged. My signal to talk faster.

"Do you take sleeping pills at night?"

Her eyebrows shot up above the rims of her sunglasses.

"Just curious," I said quickly. "Michael Girard takes pills every night to help him sleep."

Again with the eyebrows. "How would you know that?"

"I'm the president of Mr. Girard's fan club. I know *everything* about him."

I smiled winningly, but she sort of blanched, and I realized I sounded like one of those crazy stalker fans who are always getting arrested on the grounds of celebrity mansions.

"His sleeping habits came up in conversation," I said. "Because of the young woman who died the other night?"

The doors slid open, and Ava Andrews hesitated, as if weighing whether to share the elevator with me. Then she sighed and boarded, me right behind her.

"Those deaths sure put a damper on this whole event," I said. "Too bad for your brother."

She pursed her lips in a well-practiced way.

"Yes, it's too bad. Andre so wanted this film festival to be a success."

"All the media attention must've helped. The theater was full yesterday."

"Expenses have been enormous. All these VIP suites and things."

"I was wondering about that," I said. "How come you're staying at the hotel when you live right here in the Santa Fe?"

She flushed and her lips tightened. I'd touched a nerve.

"I wanted to be handy in case Andre needed me," she said. "And then there's all the media brouhaha every time I arrive someplace. I thought that would be a distraction."

I nodded, but didn't believe her for a second. The elevator slowed as we reached the lobby. I was running out of time.

"Must be nice," I said, "to be so close to Mr. Girard after all these years."

She looked me up and down, as if searching for insinuations. I kept my face blank.

"Michael is a dear friend," she said. "It was very nice of him to lend his name to this event."

"Yes," I said. "A shame how it's all turned out."

The elevator dinged. Saved by the bell, Ava Andrews squeezed through the doors and practically sprinted to the exit to get away from me. I wondered if she'd go home to her wizened husband now, or if she'd squeezed all the money out of him and left his carcass upstairs.

I went after her, but didn't make it to the front door before I was cut off by Jorge, the bouncing bellhop. His friendly smile was nowhere to be seen.

"Hey, lady. What did you say to Michael Girard?"

"What?'

"Did you tell him what I said? About the room service guy?"

"Yes, I did."

He winced.

"I thought he deserved to know there were rumors flying around."

"Are you crazy?"

"Young man. Keep a civil tongue in your head."

"Yeah?" He scowled and stepped closer. "Or what?"

"Or I will yank out that tongue and take it home as a souvenir of my stay at the Hotel Kokopelli."

I gave him my prettiest smile. He gave me some room.

"Now," I said, "you want to tell me what happened?"

"Girard called the manager about the staff spreading rumors. Threatened the hotel with lawsuits, the works. The manager's on the warpath."

Jorge looked over his shoulder, then said, "This is your fault. You don't pay for gossip, then take it directly to the person the gossip is *about*. That's not the way it works."

"I didn't know there were rules for selling rumors. Maybe I should talk to your manager. I could apologize for violating hotel protocol."

He flashed that practiced grin, but this time there was no mirth behind the mask. He barely moved his lips as he said, "Fuck off, lady."

Then he turned on his heel and stalked away.

"Same to you," I shouted after him. "You little twerp."

Chapter 42

Rather than stand around the lobby with people staring at me like I was a screeching madwoman, I went outdoors. The chill wind had picked up, swirling grit and litter in little dust devils in the corners of the hotel's entryway.

I felt I'd escaped a much bigger whirlwind inside the Hotel Kokopelli. Everyone on the gossipy staff must know by now that I was the reason Mr. Girard raised hell with the hotel management. Good thing I was checking out in the morning.

I pictured Mr. Girard on the phone with the hotel manager, his face burning as his voice got colder and colder. Who knew that my idol had the capacity for such icy anger? Not pleasant to be on the receiving end of it, as I'd learned.

Who else had he called? Attorneys and publicists and such, no doubt. His powerful friends. I wondered if he'd phoned Ava Andrews. Perhaps that was why she so abruptly left the hotel.

Too cold to just stand around, so I started walking. South, toward the Santa Fe River, the same route I'd taken with Hilda Schmidt. I strode along as if I had someplace to be, but I was lost in my thoughts.

Why would Mr. Girard feel that he needed to alert Ava Andrews to the rumors? It's not as if she--

Then it hit me. I stopped in the middle of the sidewalk, dazed. I felt like St. Paul in the Bible, knocked off my ass by an epiphany.

There *had* been a woman in Mr. Girard's room that night, and he had a good reason to hide it. She was a married woman.

Ava Andrews' suite was directly across the corridor from the one originally occupied by Mr. Girard. Pretty easy for her to slip over to see him. Carrying her nightgown in her purse.

It made sense. They'd probably been attracted to each other for years, ever since their days on "Empire." Mr. Girard remained loyal to his wife during her long illness, I felt certain. But with Lillian out of the picture, maybe Ava Andrews saw her opportunity to finally spend the night with her handsome co-star.

No accident, I'm sure, that her suite was right across the hall. She probably arranged that with her brother. Apparently, there'd been quite the little bidding war for the suites closest to Mr. Girard.

Someone bumped into me, and I turned to find that woman with the frizzy Big Bird hair. She was trying to take a picture of the sunlit clouds massing on the western horizon and had backed into me. We both apologized (though I had been standing still, minding my own business).

The encounter snapped me out of my stupor. I realized I was freezing, and got moving again, no idea where I was going, too busy trying to sort out who had been in which penthouse rooms the night that Maria Mondragon died.

Andre and Tony had a suite on that floor, but I wasn't sure where it was located. Ditto for Roger Sherwood (that rat). Kip Kaplin had wrangled the room next to Mr. Girard's. Ava Andrews *must've* heard his party, especially if she'd been tiptoeing back and forth across that hall. I wondered if she'd run into Maria Mondragon.

Good heavens, Ava Andrews could've killed Maria. Maybe she was jealous, or Maria somehow ruined Ava's big night with Mr. Girard. Ava impulsively brained her with something and, whoops, she's dead. That would've given Mr. Girard a much bigger secret to keep.

I could even see Ava luring Hilda up to the roof. How could Hilda resist such star power? A private chat under the stars with Ava Andrews? Why, that would be lovely -- whoops, splat.

Okay, I was getting carried away. But it wasn't any more implausible than the crackpot theory the police detectives were cooking up.

I paused at a corner, waiting for a break in traffic.

Two people would know for sure how the VIPs were arranged on the penthouse floor: Andre de Carlo and Tony Lodge. I checked my wristwatch. More film festival events were starting soon. I turned on my heel and made for the Zia Theater.

Chapter 43

The street in front of the theater was crowded with low-riders and dusty trucks and tourist RVs. Everybody out for a Saturday cruise, bumper to bumper at twenty miles per hour. A couple of limos were parked against the far curb, making the intersection narrower and more perilous. I waited impatiently for the "WALK" signal, then sped across. New Mexicans don't trust crosswalks. Heck, most of us don't trust walking, period. I know ranchers who drive their pickups two blocks to church.

Soon as I hopped up onto the sidewalk, the light changed and the motor parade started up again. It was a relief to enter the quiet of the theater's ornate lobby, which was empty except for a couple of stray ushers.

I pushed through the inner doors into a cavern. A movie was showing on the big screen, but it was really dark and gloomy and the actors were speaking a language I'd never heard before in my life.

By the light of the subtitles, I edged around the perimeter of the half-empty theater, searching for Tony and Andre until I was pretty sure they weren't in the audience. Probably backstage, getting ready for whatever overproduced finale Andre had dreamed up. The beefy usher guarded the doorway, just as before, and he didn't look any friendlier now.

Maybe there was an exterior door into the backstage area. You always heard about people waiting at the stage door for favorite Broadway stars to emerge. Did the Zia Theater have one? I headed for the lobby.

I pushed through the swinging doors and nearly bowled over Mitzi and Nannette. They still wore their promotional T-shirts, though both had put on black jackets (velour for Mitzi, hopsack for Nannette) against the chill, and only portions of the advertising slogans were visible. With their matching clothes and their big purses slung over their shoulders, they looked like tag-team shoppers.

Both seemed frazzled, but the wind had picked up outside and none of us wore our best coifs at the moment. The doors swung shut as we recovered from the near-collision, then we all burst into whispers.

Me: "Good God, we nearly crashed together."

Mitzi: "Yes, that was a close one!"

Nannette (sharply): "Don't you take the Lord's name in vain."

Me: "Why, I never--"

Mitzi: "Never mind. Excuse us. We shouldn't have been standing so close to the doors."

Me: "What are you doing in the lobby anyway?"

Nannette: "I don't see how that's any of your business--"

Me: "Are you *following* me again?"

Mitzi: "Don't be ridiculous, Loretta. We're not here for you. We're looking for celebrities."

Me: "Everybody's inside. The movie's still going."

Mitzi (tittering): "I can *see* that. But they'll come pouring out in a little while, and we'll be here waiting."

Me: "You really think there are any celebrities left?"

Mitzi: "You tell me. Who did you see?"

An usher approached us, a stern look on his face. Mitzi immediately charmed him into submission, of course, but by then I was going out the front door. Back out into the wind-whipped exhaust fumes of the passing traffic.

I paused at the corner to make sure the Poodles weren't trailing me, then went down the side street, searching for a stage door. A couple of blank doors were cut into the stucco wall -- fire exits, I guessed -- but they were locked to the outside world. Same story on the street that ran behind the building. Three unlabeled doors, all locked.

Hmm. This might be a bust.

I paused at the next corner, where a narrow alley led back to the busy street in front of the theater. This seemed the most likely place for a stage door, but the alley was shadowy and smelly, and I wasn't sure I wanted to traverse it alone.

It was, however, out of the wind, so I could get a few moments without my hair whipping me in the face. I stepped into the empty alley.

I found what I felt sure was the stage door, but it, too, was locked, and I wasn't about to stand around in the creepy alley until the movie let out. I walked faster, past a dumpster that reeked of urine.

With a sense of relief, I emerged from the alley, back into the sunlight and hair-ripping wind. Traffic still filled the street, moving in fits and starts. A few people loitered in front of shop windows down the block, but the sidewalk was mostly empty.

I was trying to get my hair out of my face when I heard the slap of a shoe on the cement behind me. Hands slammed into my shoulder blades, knocking me off balance, propelling me forward. I tripped off the curb and fell headlong into the street, landing on all fours, the asphalt cracking against my kneecaps and chewing up the heels of my hands.

Tires shrieked. A brown Winnebago bore down on me, smoke pouring from its locked-up wheels. Through the tall windshield, I glimpsed a wide-eyed snowbird behind the wheel, his mouth a perfect "O."

I shut my eyes tight.

Chapter 44

The screeching abruptly halted. A horn honked somewhere nearby.

I was not dead.

Coughing on the acrid smoke of burned rubber, I opened my eyes to find the front bumper mere inches away. The RV still rocked on its springs from the sudden stop.

Then excited people were all around me, shouting questions and trying to help me up. My palms were ablaze, though the shallow scrapes didn't look that bad. My jeans had protected my legs from abrasion, but I felt like I'd been kneecapped with a Louisville Slugger. I teetered as the bystanders helped me to my feet.

The white-haired driver materialized before me, his worried face inches from my own.

"My God, are you all right?"

"Yes. I think so. Just some bumps and bruises."

I held out my bleeding hands, and the sight of them made his wrinkled face pucker.

"Oh, you poor thing!" a woman shouted near my elbow. "Jesus, Stanley, you nearly ran her down!"

She was a sour-faced woman with fuzzy white hair whipped into a bun tight as a cotton swab. I took it she was the driver's wife.

"It's okay," I mumbled. "My fault. Not his."

I looked around the dozen or so people who'd gathered. Nobody I knew. Nobody who had any reason to push me into traffic. Nobody who acted like they'd seen me being pushed.

Because I *was* pushed. Make no mistake about that. Maybe nobody saw it, but it happened.

I shakily made up a story on the spot, saying my heel caught on the sidewalk, causing me to pitch into traffic. But the whole time I was spinning that concoction, my eyes searched the street and sidewalks and that shadowy alley.

Mrs. Winnebago squawked some more about how I was lucky to be alive, and how Stanley's reflexes weren't what they used to be. Now that the initial shock was wearing off, Stanley looked annoyed. Kept glancing at his wife as if he were trying to figure a way to push *her* in front of a Winnebago.

They helped me to the opposite curb. I guess we weren't moving fast enough to suit the surrounding motorists because horns started braying at us. People can be so rude.

One more round of apologies, then Stanley and wife climbed back into their giant bus and fired it up. Traffic started to move again.

After repeated assurances that I was fine, the other Good Samaritans shrugged away and left me standing on the corner, two very long blocks from my hotel. Across the street, a crowd was spilling out of the theater. People craned their necks, trying to see the cause of the traffic tie-up.

I didn't want them to see me shaken and bloodied and disheveled. I still had my pride.

I limped toward the Hotel Kokopelli, digging in my purse for Kleenex for my scraped palms, getting blood all over everything. It would've been easier if I'd stopped and paid attention to what I was doing. But I was busy watching for a killer.

Chapter 45

Cold water hitting my scraped hands made me do a little dance. My wounds weren't that bad, but, ooh, did they sting.

I sat on the closed toilet, and dug through my overnight bag until I found some Band-Aids. I covered the scrapes as best I could, but I could tell the bandages wouldn't stay long. I swallowed my last two Tylenol, and a blue pill that I found in the bottom of the bag that was either an Aleve or a Viagra.

My kneecaps throbbed, and it was a relief to sit for a minute and catch my breath.

What a close call. If that Winnebago had slid another few inches, I would've been in a hospital right now. Or a morgue. That thought made me want to call my children, but I reined myself in. It would only alarm them. They'd alert Harley. I didn't need that right now.

Because Harley was right: I *should* mind my own business. I couldn't seem to stop myself from snooping, and it had nearly gotten me killed.

I've already admitted that I can be impulsive. Harley regularly urges me to follow his plodding example and slow down and think things through first. This whole episode would prove him right once again. I looked down at my hands, crisscrossed by Band-Aids, and wondered if the scrapes would leave scars. I could use them as day-to-day reminders to practice some impulse control.

Somebody else had impulse control issues, too. The person who'd pushed me into the street. I hadn't seen anyone closing in on me while I stood on that sidewalk. Of course, I'd been looking to my left, waiting for a break in traffic, my hair in my face. Someone could've tiptoed up that alley behind me, gotten close enough to see that no one was looking. Then a quick rush. Boom, I fall into the street. And my assailant's back in that alley before anyone notices him.

Was it a him? Might've been a her. Mitzi and/or Nannette could have crept up that alley behind me. They'd been following me for days, and clearly were up to something. But if they wanted me dead, they could kill me anytime back home in Pandora. (Poison the brownies at the monthly Garden Society luncheon. I always eat too many of those.)

No, I had the sense it was a man. The rough way those hands hit me in the back, the height of my shoulder blades. A man at least as tall as me.

It wasn't planned, either. No way anyone could've predicted that I would come out of that alley when I did. No, it was an impulse. Someone saw me there at the curb, and saw the perfect opportunity. He stepped out of a doorway or out of the mouth of the alley, and shoved me into the path of that RV.

A crime of opportunity. Same as the others. No weapon, no planning, no premeditation. Just bash someone in the head with whatever's handy or push someone off a roof. Or into traffic.

An impulsive killer. Wouldn't that be the hardest kind to catch? No pattern. Unpredictable.

He'd been extremely lucky so far. Both deaths could easily be ruled accidental. If I'd been smooshed by that Winnebago, that probably would've been seen as an accident, too. That thought infuriated me. I'd be damned if I'd let him get away with it.

My hips were starting to ache from sitting on the hard toilet lid, so I moved to an armchair in the other room. The chair was turned so I could see out the window to the west, where storm clouds piled up near the horizon. I watched the ever-shifting cloudscape while my mind churned.

I thought back over the many people I'd met at the film festival, trying to think who I might've spooked with my snooping. Mr. Girard was out, since he remained under police guard, but everyone else could be a suspect. A surprisingly long inventory of people, many of whom I'd annoyed in some way. Which one would've wanted to silence me? And was it the same person who silenced Hilda?

That's why Hilda was pushed off that roof. She'd started talking. She'd told Mr. Girard about the party, but she knew something more. What could it be?

The first death, of course. Hilda knew something about how Maria Mondragon died, and she was close to telling. The killer couldn't have that, so he'd murdered Hilda, too.

That's the problem with murder. Once you start, it's hard to stop. Complications arise. Witnesses must be eliminated. Cover-ups must be maintained. Who was going to such homicidal lengths to silence people? It all went back to the night of the gala. Who killed Maria Mondragon? Who needed to cover it up?

I gasped as the answer came to me. I couldn't prove it yet, but I knew who was behind it all. The one who could least afford complications with the police. The one who had the most to lose.

Chapter 46

As I slipped out of my room, I distinctly heard a door latch click down the hall. I froze, my hand still on my doorknob, but heard nothing more. Pretty sure the noise came from the heavy door that led to the stairwell. I went the other way, toward the elevators.

I pushed the "up" button and anxiously waited, casting glances back toward the stairwell door. When the elevator dinged, I jumped again. The jerky movements were not helping my aches and pains.

The doors opened on an empty car, and I stepped inside, moving creakily on my banged-up knees. I took a deep breath and told myself I had no reason to be so nervous. It wasn't as if the killer could take another crack at me upstairs. Officer Mack still was outside Mr. Girard's door. Wasn't he?

The doors slid open, and I was relieved to see the officer at the far end of the corridor, right where I'd left him.

My gaze was snagged by movement midway down the hall. Someone disappearing into a doorway. Gray blazer, faded jeans. Good bet that it was Kip Kaplin.

I waved at the distant officer as I walked along the hall, but got the usual nothing in return. The man was a statue.

When I reached the place where I'd seen Kip, the door was still easing shut. I peeked through the crack and saw concrete stairs going up. To the roof.

I waved at the young cop again. When I had his attention, I pointed at the door and shrugged elaborately. Why go up there? He got it right away, and held two fingers up to his lips.

Ah. A place to smoke. Handy for Kip the smoker to have roof access so close to his suite. I wondered if that was part of his deal with Andre de Carlo.

I slung my purse over my shoulder, pushed open the heavy door and peeked into the stairwell. No sign of Kip. Just a dozen concrete steps up to a steel door that was slightly ajar, leaking daylight.

I looked back at Officer Mack, who was watching me, stoic as ever. Then I stepped into that stairwell.

All right, look, I'm not one of those morons you see in horror movies, who go down into the dark basement to investigate a strange noise that turns out to be an ax-wielding murderer. That's just plain stupid, and whenever I come across it in a movie or a book, it turns me right off.

Yes, I could see certain parallels to my current situation. Here I was, alone, hobbling up the stairs on my creaky knees, while a man who could very well be a killer waited at the top. However, I had no intention of going out onto that roof. I planned to take a quick peek, just to confirm that Kip was out there smoking, rather than hurling a woman off the roof or something. Then I would go to Officer Mack and demand that he radio Detectives Torres and Boyd, and I'd stand right next to him until they confronted Kip with my suspicions.

Just a quick peek. If anything went wrong, I'd scream my fool head off, and Officer Mack would come running.

Hard to be quiet on the concrete stairs when my knees didn't work properly, but I crept up them the best I could, one painful step at a time, my heart pounding all the while.

The door to the roof was propped open by a sand-colored rock the size of a mango. It was smooth like the stones that lined the bottom of the Santa Fe River, and it must've weighed two or three pounds. I pictured a hotel employee lugging it up here so he could engage in his filthy habit without locking himself out.

The flat roof was covered with tar and a thin layer of gravel littered with cigarette butts. The roof was studded with vent pipes and heating units and whatnot, and surrounded by a knee-high parapet.

Kip stood near the stucco parapet, not twenty feet away, and for once in his life he was not on the phone. He just stood there, smoking, staring not up at the fabulous orange sky, but at the street below. Thinking about Hilda, no doubt, feeling guilty. As well he should.

I had to tamp down an overwhelming urge to stalk out there and tell him off. But I'd had enough danger for one day. I'd let the authorities sort out the rest.

I took one last look at the upstart Hollywood producer, stabbing himself in the mouth with that cigarette, glaring at the world through his hipster eyeglasses. No idea what I was about to unleash upon his smarmy little--

Bam!

The door at the bottom of the stairs slammed open, startling the bejeebers out of me. Before I could turn to shush, someone hissed, "Hold it right there!"

Chapter 47

Mitzi and Nannette scowled at me from the bottom of the stairs. They still were dressed alike, and they were standing funny -- feet apart, knees flexed, elbows bent -- as if they were ready to sprint, though where they expected to run in a stairwell, I don't know. Then I realized they were striking action poses, heroines of their very own movie. Nannette had one hand buried in her leatherette handbag like a bank robber. It would've been laughable if they weren't so pathetic.

I put a finger to my lips and took a painful step downward. They both flinched, as if I, Loretta Kimball, a forty-nine-year-old homemaker they've both known since elementary school, might suddenly leap down the stairwell at them, teeth bared.

"What is *wrong* with you?" I whispered. "What are you doing here?"

"Exactly what I was going to ask you," Mitzi said, speaking in her usual whinny.

I pointed back over my shoulder with my thumb.

"Somebody's out there," I whispered. "I don't want him to hear us."

"Who? Who is it?"

"Do you not know how to whisper? Did they never teach you that in kindergarten?"

"No reason why *we* should whisper," Nannette snapped. "*We've* got nothing to hide."

"What the hell is that supposed to mean?"

"What are you doing in this stairwell, Loretta?" Mitzi said. At least she was keeping her voice down now. "Planning to push someone *else* off the roof?"

I couldn't have been more dumbfounded if they'd walloped me with a dead cat. Push somebody off the roof? Me?

"Let's see for ourselves," Mitzi said. "Open that door. We'll all go out there."

"We can't." I glanced back at the door. "Kip's out there."

"Who?"

"The movie producer," I whispered. "With the glasses?"

Blank stares.

"I think he's the killer."

Nannette and Mitzi exchanged a smug look, as if they could see right through me, then Mitzi said, "Open that door, Loretta."

"We don't want to go out there," I whispered furiously. "He's the one who--"

"*Now!*" Nannette hissed.

"No." I crossed my arms over my chest. "It's too dangerous."

"More dangerous in here."

Nannette pulled her hand out of her purse and showed me a little black pistol.

"Good heavens," I said. "Is that real?"

"Yes, it's real," she said. "I've got a permit for it, and I know how to use it."

"You wouldn't shoot me."

Her lipless mouth curved into an unfamiliar smile. "Just try me."

"I'll scream."

"If you do, I'll shoot you."

"You'll get arrested."

"You'll get dead."

That shut me up. If it had been Mitzi (or most anyone else) making the threats, I wouldn't have believed it. Not with a policeman down the hall. But, as everyone in Pandora knows, Nannette Hoch is crazy as a shithouse rat. She might pull the trigger just to see what happens.

"All right," I said aloud, weary of whispering. "But watch out for Kip."

"Don't worry about us," Mitzi said. "We've got this situation under control."

I rolled my eyes so hard, it's a wonder I didn't sprain them.

"You've both lost your cotton-pickin' minds."

Nannette apparently was done talking. She jabbed the gun in my direction to get me moving, then she and Mitzi came up the stairs behind me, staying just out of reach. (Believe me, a swift kick crossed my mind. I held the high ground.)

I paused at the door and peered through the crack. Kip still smoked by the parapet, twenty feet away. As I watched, he dropped the cigarette to the gravel and stepped on the butt.

I hesitated. Last chance to call for help. But I got a look at the fanatical gleam in Nannette's eyes, and decided it would be better to step outside into the wind.

The sun had slipped behind the massing clouds, which were yellow and orange edged with red, like a bowl of fresh-cut peaches. So beautiful it made my breath catch in my throat, and I thought, at least I have this last New Mexico sunset.

Kip turned at the sound of the door opening, and seemed surprised to see three women march out onto the roof with him, gravel crunching underfoot. Guess he hadn't heard us in the stairwell over the gusting wind, which now snatched at our clothes and hair.

Nannette was last through the door, which banged against the river rock that kept it ajar. She showed Kip her pistol.

"Come here, you," she said. "We need to talk."

Kip's feet did a little dance before he could get them under control and walk over to us.

"What the hell?" he said. "What's the gun for?"

"Shut up and listen."

Nannette gestured for Mitzi to go ahead. Mitzi straightened her spine and cleared her throat, just the way she'd learned in Public Speaking 101, and said, "Nannette and I have been busy little investigators the past few days. A regular Holmes and Watson."

I managed not to snort.

"Ever since that first girl was killed," she continued, "we've suspected you."

I looked over at Kip, who'd gone ashen.

"So we started following you," Mitzi said, and, whoa, I realized she was not speaking to Kip. She was talking to *me*.

"Wait a minute. You thought *I* had something to do with--"

"Shut it!" Nannette said with enough ferocity that I immediately complied. "Let her finish."

"We knew you were jealous of Maria Mondragon," Mitzi said.

"*What*?"

"We saw you at the gala. You spotted that young woman flirting with Michael Girard, and jealousy was written all over your face."

"Are you nuts?" I said. "Harley was standing *right there* at the time."

"Doesn't matter," Nannette snapped. "Jealousy was in your heart. We could tell."

In frustration, I slapped a hand to my forehead, forgetting about my scrapes and Band-Aids. The pain lit me right up, but I still managed to hear every word Mitzi said.

"Ever since Maria Mondragon was killed, you've been skulking around and sneaking up on people. Covering your tracks. Hilda must've figured it out, so you had to get rid of her, too. You were friends. She would've come up on this roof with you."

I shook my head. These two idiots had misinterpreted everything they'd seen. No wonder I couldn't turn around without finding them at my heels.

The four of us still stood near the propped-open door, and Kip suddenly took a step in that direction.

"I'm sure the police would like to hear this theory," he said. "I'll go get that cop downstairs."

Mitzi stepped between him and the door. "I'm not done yet."

Kip tried smiling at her, but it flickered like a dying marquee.

"Look," he said, "I don't understand all this, exactly, but it's pretty clear you don't need me here. This is between the three of you, and the police, and I really don't want to get involved."

"Don't listen to him!" I shouted, which got Nannette to aim her pistol at me again. I wished she'd stop pointing it at people.

"I'm on probation in California," Kip said. "No big deal, a minor drug thing. But I can't have any brushes with the law."

I risked getting shot to shout over him. "That's it! That's what this is all about!"

The three of them gaped at me.

"*Kip* is the one who's been covering things up," I said. "He couldn't afford to get arrested. He'd get sent straight to prison."

The other two looked at him.

"This is preposterous," he said, "and I won't be a party to it. I'm going to get that cop."

He stepped around Mitzi, headed for the door, but Nannette cut him off.

"You're not going anywhere," she snarled. "Not until Loretta has had her say."

That surprised me. I didn't expect to be given a turn. Nannette might be insane, but she was fair.

Mitzi seemed surprised, too.

"Um, sure," she said. "Go ahead, Loretta."

Before they could change their minds, I took a deep breath and started talking as fast as I could. I sounded like a livestock auctioneer, but I had a lot of ground to cover.

"Maria Mondragon was in Kip's suite the night she died. Hilda was there, too. At a party he hosted with his pal Sean Hyde. They were drinking and doing drugs. In direct violation of Kip's probation, I might add."

His cheeks flushed.

"Maria got so out of it that she fell and hit her head, probably on one of those sharp-edged granite sinks in the bathroom."

I still wasn't entirely sure that was how it happened, but the surprise in Kip's eyes suggested I was on the right track.

"The rest of them probably didn't even notice," I said. "They were having a high old time. But finally somebody realized Maria had been in the bathroom a long time."

His mouth fell open. Now I was certain I had it right.

"They panicked. Kip can't call the police, not when the autopsy will show Maria was full of drugs. So they had to get rid of the body."

"Really," he interrupted. "This is getting--"

"Shut it!" Nannette jabbed the pistol toward Kip's crotch. He clammed up.

"Mr. Girard's suite was next door," I said, "and Hilda had a key. Somehow, Kip persuaded her it would go easier for everybody if the body was found there."

"That's crazy," Mitzi said. "Michael Girard's a big celebrity."

"But he's got a flawless reputation," I said. "Hilda must've thought he could weather the storm."

"Unbelievable."

"They weren't thinking straight," I said. "Remember, they'd been partying for hours. So they hauled Maria next door and left her on the sofa. The next morning, they woke up to find a media firestorm."

Okay, that was a little dramatic, but Mitzi and Nannette nodded right along. They'd done their share of wading through photographers the past few days.

"Kip kept cornering Hilda, warning to her to keep quiet. Plus, he was greedy. He still wanted her to sell Mr. Girard on doing his Western."

From the flush on Kip's face, I could tell I'd scored another direct hit.

"Hilda couldn't take the pressure. She wanted to confess everything. Kip lured her up here to talk it over. They smoked a little weed. Then, once she relaxed, he shoved her off the roof."

"Oh, I did not--"

"Shut it!"

"*Then*," I said, "after *I* started asking questions, he tried to get rid of me, too. He pushed me into traffic today. I was almost hit by an RV!"

I held out my bandaged hands as proof, and they leaned over to examine them.

Kip saw his chance. While we were distracted, he charged Nannette, lowering his shoulder and slamming her into the steel stairwell door. It was still propped open by the river rock, and the crash echoed in the stairwell.

Before she could recover, Kip wrested the pistol from Nannette and pushed her away. He got the gun turned around in his hands, so he had us covered. He'd lost his glasses in the tussle, and his breath was coming hard, but what he said came through loud and clear: "I should kill all three of you meddling bitches."

Chapter 48

I was the first one to regain her wits.

"Need I remind you," I said, "that there's a policeman at the bottom of the stairs? You shoot us, and you'll never get out of here alive."

"Might be worth it," he said, "just to get some peace and quiet."

Mitzi, as usual, chose the worst time to chime in. "You'll get plenty of peace and quiet in prison!"

Kip reached back with his free hand and pulled open the stairwell door. The pistol roved back and forth, its muzzle an ebony eye keeping watch over us. He looked down just long enough to push the rock out of the way with his foot.

"Talk all you want out here on the roof," he said. "By the time someone hears you, I'll be long gone."

He turned and hurried down the stairs.

The heavy door was swinging shut, but I lunged and caught the edge just before it closed. Nearly smashed my fingers, but I'd risk my whole hand to avoid being trapped on a roof with the Poodles.

I yanked open the door, spilling sunlight down the stairwell. Kip was nearly to the bottom of the stairs. He wasn't looking back at us, too busy watching where he put his feet.

Without a moment's hesitation (or forethought), I scooped up that smooth stone and launched it down the stairwell after him.

Stupid, I know. Impulsive. That heavy rock could've hit him in the head and killed him on the spot. Worse, it could've missed, and made him mad enough to come back upstairs and shoot us.

But I was lucky. The stone tumbled through the air and hit him right between the shoulder blades. The impact knocked him off his feet and he went flying into the heavy door at the bottom.

Well. It was like running headfirst into a wall. Kip crumpled into a pile at the bottom of the stairs. Out cold.

Ever the cheerleader, Mitzi shouted, "Yay!"

I didn't wait to hear Nannette's reaction. I was too busy limping down the stairs to get that pistol. I didn't want it to fall into the Poodles' paws again.

"Loretta!" Mitzi called after me, but I ignored her.

I reached the bottom step, and Kip hadn't so much as twitched. The pistol was on the floor, too near his hand for my comfort. I tiptoed around him, and nimbly picked up the little black gun.

The hallway door flew open so suddenly, it's a wonder I didn't shoot myself in the foot.

Officer Mack filled the doorway, his hand on the butt of his holstered pistol.

We must've made a pretty picture. Kip sprawled unconscious on the floor. Me standing over him, a pistol in my bandaged hands. And two crazy women at the top of the stairs, babbling in fear.

"Drop the gun," Mack commanded.

He didn't have to tell me twice.

Chapter 49

It was nearly midnight by the time I got back to my room. I was too tired to post anything to the fan club website, too tired to even call Harley. (He'd get the whole story soon enough. Probably take the whole three-hour drive back to Pandora to tell it all.)

I just wanted to go to bed.

Detectives Boyd and Torres had made me go through my story a dozen times, and their questions still ricocheted inside my head. But they'd believed me in the end, and that was what mattered. Kip Kaplin was under arrest.

Well, technically, he was in the hospital with a dislocated shoulder and a pretty serious concussion, so he wasn't going anywhere anyway. But the detectives had assured me he would be charged with murder, and a guard would be placed outside his hospital room. I hoped it wasn't Officer Mack. He'd had enough excitement for one week.

Nannette wasn't charged with anything, though I tried to persuade the police that she was a danger to herself and others. Since it all turned out well, they seemed willing to overlook the fact that she pulled a gun on an innocent person. The police did confiscate her pistol as evidence, and that news should come as a relief to everyone in Llano County.

The Poodles would get what's coming to them, just as soon as I got home. I could hardly wait to tell Inez and everyone else in Pandora how the two amateur sleuths had tried to pin the murders on me. The town could use a good laugh. For once, I'd outshined Mitzi Tyner. It was only fair that everyone in Pandora knew about it.

But for now, I was one exhausted heroine. I stepped out of my shoes as soon as I entered my room, and shucked clothes all the way to the bathroom. After all the gabbing and stale coffee, my mouth felt furry, and I spent a long time brushing my teeth and staring at my disheveled reflection in the mirror.

Bathroom lighting is always so harsh, it's no wonder so many people commit suicide in hotels. Granted, I was not at my best, but that was definitely a fifty-year-old woman staring back at me. She looked weary.

I slipped into a sleeping shirt decorated with kittens. (The cats pajamas. Get it? Never mind.) Then I got under the lusciously thick covers and melted into the bed.

Ah.

Someone rapped lightly on the door.

"Oh, for shit's sake." I wrestled my way out of bed and turned on a lamp and located the white hotel bathrobe. It barely reached my knees, but it would do the job while I told off whatever heartless wretch still tapped on my door.

I hobbled over to the door and yanked it open, ready to unload on the hapless knocker.

There stood Michael Girard.

"Sorry to disturb you so late," he said. "The detectives told me you'd just come up."

I was so flabbergasted, I could barely find the words to ask him in. It was a little awkward as I held the door open for him. He passed so close, I could smell his hair tonic.

Even more awkward once we were in the room together. The bedcovers were tossed back, the light was low, and I was in my pajamas. Mr. Girard stopped next to the desk and gestured toward a dark lamp.

"May I?"

I nodded, and he switched on the lamp. Then he smoothly pulled out the desk chair for me. While I sat and tucked my robe around my knees, he dragged over an armchair so he could sit facing me.

"I owe you an apology," he said. "I was quite rude to you before. It seems you had my best interests at heart all along."

"Oh, Mr. Girard, you don't have to apologize. I understand you've been under enormous pressure."

He shook his regal head. "Doesn't excuse bad behavior. Good manners aren't conditional."

See why I've always admired this man? What a class act.

"I'm afraid I haven't been at my best throughout this whole affair," he said. "I feel terrible about my last conversation with Hilda. Though murder is horrible, it's a relief to know she didn't kill herself because of what I said."

"She thought the world of you, Mr. Girard."

"I should've done more to warn her away from Kip Kaplin. I had a bad feeling about him from the start."

Nothing much I could say to that. I simply nodded.

"Is it true that you brained him with a *rock*?"

"Not exactly. I threw it at him. It was the only thing handy."

I gave him a brief rundown of what happened on the roof. When I finished, Mr. Girard shook his head.

"You're lucky to be alive. And the other two women? They're okay?"

"Physically, yes. Mentally, no. But that was always the case."

He laughed. "A couple of kooky Sherlocks. But you were the real detective. You seem to be quite a capable woman."

"I've raised two children and sent them to college. After that, most everything seems doable."

"You know," he said, that twinkle in his blue eyes, "I'm going to need a new assistant to replace Hilda. Ever thought about living in Hollywood?"

I could tell he wasn't serious, but I still had to pause and remember how to breathe.

"Thank you, Mr. Girard, but I couldn't possibly. My place is with my husband in Pandora. I'm needed there."

He gave me a wink (which nearly stopped my heart), and said, "I knew you'd say that. You're very loyal."

"Loyalty's like good manners," I said. "It's not conditional. True friends remain loyal in the face of all hardships and indiscretions."

The smile slipped from his face, and he studied me in silence. I knew he was thinking about his own indiscretion with a married woman. I hadn't mentioned to the police or anyone else that I suspected Ava Andrews had been in Mr. Girard's suite that night. I had no evidence, and saw no reason to stir up more gossip. But he could tell I knew.

"For our friends," he said, "we overlook bad behavior. And still come to their rescue when they need it."

"That's right."

"That makes you quite the true friend, Loretta. I'm walking around a free man, thanks to you."

Blushing, I told him he was ever so welcome, and reminded him that he still owed me an interview.

"I'd be delighted. Anytime."

We got to our feet, and I held out my bandaged hand for him to shake.

His hand was warm and soft as it clasped mine. He looked me right in the eyes, thrilling me to my toes. Then he turned my hand in his and, never breaking the eye-lock with me, bent and kissed it.

The touch of his lips sent an electric charge up my arm, right to my brain, which responded by turning to oatmeal.

"Oh, my."

One last blast of his dazzling smile, and I nearly swooned. Then he turned and glided out the door without a backward glance.

A gentleman to the end.

Made in the USA
Coppell, TX
26 January 2024

28248203R00180